PRELUDE TO A BLOOD ENCOUNTER

It was a shock to see him. He had been an unseen presence for such a long time, it was as though I had never been face to face with him before. He didn't look as crazy as I expected him to— maybe not as crazy as I looked at that moment. He didn't even look savage . . . Just old Cousin Jim Otis Churchwarden, with the easy smile and always engaging manner. That same fun-loving friendly twinkle must have been on his lips when he leaped on the hood of that Mercury and shot Leona Blye Churchwarden and her boyfriend. It must have been the last thing that she saw. And it might be the last thing that I saw.

THE KILLING PLACE

Tad Richards

A DELL BOOK

Published by
Dell Publishing Co., Inc.
1 Dag Hammarskjold Plaza
New York, New York 10017

Dell ® TM 681510, Dell Publishing Co., Inc.
Printed in the United States of America
First printing—December 1976

CHAPTER 1

"You remember your cousin Jim Otis Churchwarden, don't you?" my mother asked in her letter. *"Of course you do. He was such a favorite of all you boys when you were younger, with those outlandish ways of his."*

That was always my mother's style. She knew I hadn't thought about anybody in Clove Valley since I'd left the mountains for good, five years ago, and moved to Washington, D.C., but she'd never admit it. So every letter I got from her was the same: "You remember" so-and-so, and such-and-such, and this place or the other, or the time when this or that happened—"of course you do." And then she'd go ahead and refresh my memory, because of course most of the time I didn't. And about three quarters of the time it was some sort of cousin, too. Ma had the bloodlines of Passaqua County worked out right down to the last tenth cousin three times removed, and anyone who was even remotely related to us got a relative credit in her letters, even if they were people I'd never heard of.

I was reading this letter out loud to some of my
D.C. friends at a party. The party was at these two
stewardesses' place. I'd taken out one of them a few
times. She was a brunette with a great figure, but I
hadn't been able to score with her yet. She was kind
of prudish, I guess. But her roommate was pretty
wild, and she threw some outrageous parties. They
used to smoke pot there a whole lot, and one time I
remember there was even some cocaine. They got a
little worried about me when I got this new job as a
federal marshal, but I told them not to sweat about
that. I sure wasn't going to go around busting people I
knew right and left for smoking pot, even if I had the
jurisdiction. I didn't really think of myself as a cop,
anyway. It was just something I was doing while I got
it together to go to law school.

Anyway, I was reading this letter from Ma. Most of
the people I hung around with knew I came from that
part of the country, and at first I was kind of embarrassed about it, my hillbilly accent and all; but then I
started making a joke of it. It was always a good way
to break the ice with a chick, anyway. And some of
the letters I got from home really were pretty funny,
just like Charlie Weaver, except for real.

"What sort of outlandish ways did he have?" asked
this tall redheaded girl whom I sort of had my eye on.
She was a stewardess, too, just visiting in town from the
West Coast. And the last chick visiting in town from
the West Coast at one of these parties had ended up
giving blow jobs on the living-room floor after I'd left
the party, so I didn't want to take a chance on missing
out with this one.

I grinned at her. "Well, he was a moonshiner for a start," I told her. "He had two or three stills up in the mountains, so he always had a piece of money in his jeans. And he knew how to soup up a car so it made more noise and took off faster than anything else in three counties. And he really knew how to snow the girls. All us younger guys wanted to learn that from him."

"Did he pass on any of his secrets to you?" asked the redhead.

I could feel the brunette's eyes burning into my neck, but what the hell. I wasn't getting anything from her. And you either move when the moving's good, or you don't.

"All of them," I said, fixing her with my most straight-ahead seductive stare.

"What else does dear old Ma have to say about Cousin Jim?" asked the brunette.

"Cousin Jim Otis," I corrected.

"And did you have two names when you were a li'l ol' mountain boy?" she purred.

That really made me mad. It was one thing for me to kid about it, but I hated it when anyone else kidded me. Anyway, I ignored her and went on with the letter.

"Well, Cousin Jim Otis finally went and did it. After all these years of being the most eligible bachelor in Passaqua County, right when we'd all just about given up on him, he went and tied the knot.

"You remember your Cousin Zena Blye, that used to be Zena Glascoe? Of course you do. She and her hus-

band, Bill Ed, have that old dirt farm ten miles north
of Clove Valley, up near the Gap. Anyway, they've
been having their share of troubles, as haven't we all,
and it looked for a spell like they were going to lose
the farm to the bank, but Jim Otis helped them out,
and, well, first thing you know he was visiting them at
the farm a lot, and we all thought maybe he was 'ca-
shaying' some of that sinful moonshine whiskey he
makes out at Bill Ed's, when surprise! They up and
announce that Jim Otis and Leona, the youngest Blye
girl, were planning a wedding! Did you ever hear the
like? You remember your cousin Leona, don't you? Of
course you do. Naturally, she was just a little girl
when you went away, but she's all of thirteen now,
and real 'advanced' for her age, they say."

I stopped a minute for breath—I guess you'd call it
more of a dramatic pause, because naturally I was expecting a reaction about then, and naturally I got it.

"Thirteen!" gasped the redhead. "How advanced
could she be?"

"About four or five months advanced, I'll bet," said
my pal Eddie.

There were shrieks of laughter. Eddie really had a
way with a quip.

"Wait—wait till I get on to the wedding itself," I
said.

"The wedding was last Saturday, and that Jim
Otis—well, he is a 'caution' and no mistake. You know
he couldn't get married without turning it into the
'event' of the year, and of course, he had to be the

'star.' I declare, with Jim Otis Churchwarden at the wedding, you wouldn't have even known the bride was there if she hadn't 'a been wearing white.

"Jim Otis had the whole 'shebang'—wedding and reception both—out at Wheeler's field, and there must have been a hundred or more people there. He had one of them 'new-fangled' country music bands down from Waynesville, with those plug-in guitars that make so much noise you can't think over them. And he got up and played his banjo too—you remember how nice he can play when he sets to it?—of course you do—when he wasn't dancing with every female person in sight, child to grandmother."

"Probably propositioned every pea-pickin' one of them, too," someone cracked.

"And when he wasn't dancing, he was shaking hands, clapping people on the back, and playing practical jokes. I bet he must have given a dozen 'hot-foots' to people if he gave one. Oh, and making sure everyone's glass was full. There certainly was a lot of drinking-liquor 'flowing' at that party, and if the truth be known, I misdoubt if there was ever a cent of whiskey tax paid on any of it. But no one would have the heart to question a man about a 'ticklish' subject like that on his wedding day, and I believe that half the law officers of the state were at the party, 'drinking it up,' anyway. Even your father, bless him, got a little 'tipsy,' and started doing a 'jig,' or something, with old Aunt Martha Lupton. You remember her, don't you? Of course you do. Your father's aunt, the *deaf one that you always had to say everything twice to.*

"And then Jim Otis—I guess he must have had his 'share' to drink by this time, too—he jumped up on the bandstand and started making a speech through that microphone about what a great lover he was, and all about how many girls would have broken hearts tonight, and then he started going on about what he was going to do on his wedding night—'if you think this party is something, you oughta see what's going to come after,' was just one of the things he said, and I don't think I ought to write down the rest on a piece of paper, not one that has to be sent through the mail—I declare, if I'd 'a been your cousin Leona, I think I would have 'died' from the shame.

"Oh, but the most 'outrageous' thing of all was when T.J. Atkins—you remember T.J.? Of course you do. You used to steal apples off his tree on your way to school before they got that new 'central' school and put the school bus in. Anyway, old T.J. had himself just a little too much of that 'white lightning,' I guess, and it seemed like he didn't know just exactly where he was. Anyway, he went over behind a bush to relieve himself, but he kind of staggered around the bush and ended up on the side facing all the people. Well, he started to take down his pants, and you know how fat he is—well, there just these two great big round 'cheeks' just as plain as plain, right out in the open, just staring at everyone. Quick as a flash, Jim Otis picks up his shotgun that's in the front seat of his pickup loaded with birdshot, and . . ."

I couldn't go on. Eddie was just roaring with laughter. He was lying on the floor, choking and gasping for breath, and everyone else was laughing too. So was I.

"Can you imagine . . . he must still be picking buckshot out of his ass," someone gasped.

"Yeah—and what about his wedding night—I wonder what else he said about it?"

"Maybe he promised to fuck her once for every year old she was, like at a birthday party."

I'd managed to work my way around to sitting down next to the redhead by this point, and as I laughed I laid my hand on her knee to steady myself, and left it there. She was roaring with laughter, too, her eyes glistening and her bosom heaving. She looked very receptive.

"Maybe you missed your big chance by leaving home, Ryland," said the brunette. "A man of your gifts—why the thirteen-year-olds should take to you like a pig to mud."

I removed my hand from the redhead's knee, like a coward. But I was getting angry, too. "I can do just fine for myself up here, thank you," I said.

"Oh, I'm sure you can," she said in a silky voice. "But I can't help wondering what would happen if some day your primal cultural instincts were to just . . . take over. I mean, there you are, striding down the halls of the Justice Department, and suddenly a junior high school class passes by on a school field trip, and this really cute little eighth-grader winks at you—"

"*Shut up!*" I shouted, surprising even myself with

the vehemence of my anger. Suddenly none of it seemed very funny anymore.

Actually, I knew deep inside I had never thought any of it was very funny. That was just something I did to pretend to myself that none of them were real people. To pretend that people I knew and grew up with and had for parents and relatives—that I was almost one of—were storybook characters who did things like that. They married girls who were only thirteen years old. They got drunk on cheap rotgut whiskey and fired off guns at each other during weddings.

It wasn't funny at all, not to me. It made me want to throw up.

I ended up going home with the redhead, though. But as it turned out, she wasn't too good in the sack. Not what I'd heard West Coast chicks were like. And I didn't get invited back to another party at those two stewardesses' place for a long time, either.

Things didn't go too well for my cousin Jim Otis and his child bride, either, apparently. The next thing I heard from Ma was that about a month and a half after the wedding, Leona had left him and gone to stay with relatives in Greenbush, in the next state. At least Ma didn't ask me if I remembered-them-of-course-I-did. I guess she didn't know them either.

I got the next installment of the story from the Justice Department wires. It was that two bodies, identified as those of Leona Blye Churchwarden, thirteen, of Clove Valley, and Kenneth McCluen, seventeen, of Greenbush, had been found in a parked car on a deserted road about four miles east of Greenbush. They had been shot at close range with a 12-gauge shotgun. The principal suspect, still at large, was the murdered girl's husband, James Otis Churchwarden.

CHAPTER 2

Jim Otis Churchwarden was presumed to have fled back across the state line into Passaqua County, and the state police expected to pick him up within twenty-four hours. And I was given my first real assignment as a marshal. I was sent down by the Marshal's Office to transport him into custody back to the state where he was wanted.

I suppose I could have begged off the assignment on the grounds that he was my cousin. But that didn't seem right on my first job. And besides, I didn't think that anyone except my mother could explain exactly how that relationship worked out.

And anyway, I guess I figured it was about time I paid a visit to the folks. I hadn't been home in five years, not even for Thanksgiving or Christmas, and without some outside reason for going down there, probably another five years would go by, and even then probably I'd never do it. So this seemed like as good a chance as any. I'd go back home at the government's expense, pop in on the folks, then pick up Jim Otis and take him over to the authorities in Greenbush. I'd have a perfect excuse for going down, and a perfect excuse for not staying longer.

I made plans to be away from Washington for about a week. I asked my building super to pick up my mail and hold it for me. I didn't have a girl friend at the moment, so I asked Eddie to take care of my cat till I got back. That's kind of an imposition on a male friend, but Eddie was cool about it.

We exchanged a few jokes about hillbilly shotgun freaks and feuds and so on, and he asked me which side I would take if the Blyes and the Churchwardens got into a family feud, seeing as how I was related to both of them. I couldn't think of a really swift comeback for that, so I just laughed. What else was I going to do? I didn't want to start talking about how there hadn't been a murder in Passaqua County in the last thirty years, because if I started defending them, it would sound too much like I was identifying with them.

Besides, I reflected on my way to the airport, I would have had to qualify that with: "except for the two revenue agents who got killed up in the mountains about twelve years ago." Eddie would have gotten a big belt out of that. I could just hear him— "*revenooers*, eh?"—mimicking and exaggerating my accent. I laughed as I thought of it.

But now I was a federal agent too.

I rented a car in the state capital and drove up to Waynesville, where the state police barracks in Passaqua County was located. And it was then that I discovered that there had been a slight last-minute snag in the plans. They hadn't picked up Jim Otis yet.

I went up to Waynesville, where the state police headquarters were, first. I talked to Captain Falkner of the BCI. Jim Otis had slipped through their dragnet for the moment and was still at large, but they were confident he was still in the area, and they weren't expecting any trouble in finding him and picking him up. Captain Falkner advised me to just sit tight for a few days. He understood I was a local boy—why didn't I go home and spend some time with the folks, and he'd let me know when there was a break in the case.

While I was there, he showed me all the dossiers they had on the case, and on Jim Otis.

Description, which I knew well enough. White male, 36 years old, 5 feet 11 inches, 170 pounds. Sandy hair, blue eyes. Tattoo, left bicep: *Born To Make Out*. Close-cropped mustache when last seen.

Fingerprints. Previous arrests: a few disturbing the peace, one assault, one moonshining—three months in the county jail for that one, then the rest of the sentence suspended.

Armed, considered dangerous.

Details on the killings: two bodies, identified as Leona Churchwarden, thirteen, and Kenneth McCluen, seventeen, shot at close range, etc. Positive identification of the bodies made by the victims' mothers.

"Hell of a thing to have to put a mother through," I said.

Captain Falkner nodded. "Take a look at the pictures."

The photographs showed an old car, a '57 Mercury Comet, with its windshield completely shattered as if from a head-on collision. And the two bodies on the front seat—well, you had to look closely to be sure that there were two bodies. They had been blown into one mangled, bloody heap, and the only thing left to count by was the legs.

There were two pairs. A boy's legs, hairy and knobby, with his jeans pulled all the way off on one side, and rolled down around his ankle and work boot on the other. And a girl's legs. That would be my cousin Leona, as Ma would say. My cousin—though I'd never met her, or even heard of her that I could remember, before this whole Jim Otis thing. I didn't even know what she looked like.

And I'd never know, not from these pictures. As with the boy, just legs. And they were bare, like his. The skirt that must have been rolled up to her waist was tattered and drowned in blood and guts and pulp.

All you could tell about her from her legs was how young she was. They were still skinny, not yet rounded and shapely like a woman's, not much calf or ankle to them. Bobby sox on her feet and one sneaker.

And yes, the two bodies were joined together at the waist. He hadn't given them time to roll apart.

I closed the folder. I had never seen anything like those photographs. I felt like I was about to throw up.

Captain Falkner started talking again, quickly, and I was grateful for that.

"Looks like he must have leaped right up on the hood, and fired straight down through the windshield. Maybe they never even knew what hit them. Or it could be . . ." The captain paused for a moment. My hand involuntarily twitched back to the folder and flipped it open to reveal the death pictures again. The captain drew a breath, but when he resumed speaking there was no dramatic emphasis except in my mind— his voice was as flat and professional and unemotional as it had been before.

" . . . that they got frozen together by panic, and just couldn't pull loose."

I slapped the folder shut again, hard. But my eyes had to have something to fasten on, to keep them from being drawn back again and again to that horrible, mesmerizing tableau. I opened the other folder again, and concentrated hard on a photograph of Jim Otis Churchwarden.

It was a big eight-by-ten glossy, from the files of the Waynesville *Patriot*. It showed Jim Otis, wearing a white studded Eisenhower-length jacket, his hair greased back in an Elvis Presley-style pompadour, standing on a bandstand, his hand raised as if to quiet an audience, and an insouciant grin on his lips. I guessed it must have been taken at the wedding.

Was that what he looked like when he jumped on the hood of that Mercury Comet, shotgun in hand? Did he stare in the window, grinning like he was up on stage telling tall tales about his wedding night, or was his face twisted with passion and rage? Or had he turned his face away, unable at the last minute to look straight ahead at the destruction he was causing? What was the last sight those two teenagers had seen as they lay together looking up through the windshield, too frozen with terror to pull apart? I tried hard to picture the scene, horrible as it was, in a vain attempt to get that other picture out of my mind, but it was no use. Later, though, driving home, all the pictures, the ones seen and the ones imagined, would come flooding back over me, and I would have to stop at a roadhouse and try to drink my imagination into oblivion on 3.2 beer.

I had a feeling I wasn't acting very much like a hardened professional law enforcement officer, but there was nothing I could do about it. I did ask Captain Falkner one question before I left, swallowing hard and trying to work some moisture into my mouth to prevent my voice from coming out as a cracked squeak: "Was she pregnant?"

"About three weeks," he said.

My parents' house was up on a little hill, behind my father's general store, so it was right in town. In fact, my dad's store *was* the town—it and the post office.

I went to the store first. It was empty when I walked in. The bells on the door jingled when it opened, but no one came out front.

There was no particular need to come out front, by my Dad's philosophy. If it was just a farmer, say, come for his plug of tobacco, or a housewife to pick up a bottle of ammonia and a box of cereal for the kids, they could just take it off the shelves and leave the money on the counter for him. Or, if the lady wanted, say, a pound of flour measured out, all she had to do was call out, "Mr. Justice!" and in a minute or so he would come bustling out into the front, a short, plump but frail-looking gentleman in loose-fitting khaki clothes from the Army surplus store and a white apron, always brusque but sociable.

It just didn't seem like the right way to run a business, to me. Not that I thought anyone in Clove Valley would steal anything from the store, but—I don't know. Maybe he could have been more of a salesman, encouraged people to buy more, if he spent more time out in front and on the job.

Instead he was in the back, where there were tables and benches, and where the local men sat and drank beer, and chewed tobacco, and talked about hunting and fishing, and played euchre.

There was also a dance floor in the back. It was separated from the tables and benches that surrounded it on two sides by a low partition, and it had an old jukebox that played 78 RPM records. The jukebox played one song for a nickel, three for a dime. You put your nickel or dime into the flat tray with the right-sized indentation on it, jammed it back into the machine with the heel of your hand, and the turntable would rise up to rest under the record you had selected from the titles clumsily lettered in block capitals, each word separated by a dash, next to the selection buttons. As far back to my earliest childhood as I could remember, there had always been the same old corny, horribly scratchy records: "SHRIMP-BOATS," "HONEY-BABE," "I'M-MOVIN-ON," "THE-YELLOW-ROSE-OF-TEXAS," "MOCKINBIRD-HILL," "BACK-IN-THE-SADDLE-AGAIN," "I'VE-GOT-SPURS-THAT-JINGLE-JANGLE-JINGLE," "THE-BALLAD-OF-DAVY-CROCKETT"—I could probably still reel off all thirty of them from memory, and I can still never hear any of those songs, anywhere, without being overcome by a vague sinking sensation and feeling the hackles start to rise on the back of my neck.

They had square dances at the store on Saturday nights. Everybody in Clove Valley always went to them, and there would be a band that always seemed to have a tall, skinny fiddler in a string tie who held his fiddle in the crook of his arm and did the calling, and a plump, blonde lady in a red dress who played the accordion and did some of the singing. They were always up there, doing it, Saturday night after Saturday night, as far back as I can remember. I don't even know if they were always the same people.

And the sets were always made up of toothless old men dancing with embarrassed young girls, and big fat ladies dancing with skinny men, and even bigger, fatter ladies dancing with little boys.

Were all the ladies in Clove Valley really that huge, or did I just remember it that way? In all that country of dirt farmers and miners, all those men who made their living with their backs and arms every day, were all the women really that much bigger and stronger? All I know for sure is that every woman who ever picked me up and dragged me out onto the floor to be her square dance partner was at least seven feet tall, and had biceps the size of smoked hams, and bosoms like boxing gloves. When I started going to central school in seventh grade, we had to take square dancing twice a week for gym in the winter, but at least there it was all right to hate it; and besides, you could tell the girls what you thought of them. But when some big old friend of your mother's came and grabbed you by the collar and took your hand and led

you out to the dance floor at the store, you had to go
along with it and act like you liked it or catch Holy
Hell from Ma. And my mother was the biggest and
strongest old lady I'd ever seen.

Oh, I'm a really good dancer now. I can do the boo-
galoo, and the funky chicken, and whatever else is
new—I can pick it up in one evening. But not square
dancing. And not with anyone over 105 pounds.

I went into the back room to see Pa. He was sitting
at a table playing euchre with Skipper Storey; and if
he was glad to see me, it didn't excite him enough to
tear him away from his game. He squinted at his
hand, played a trump, and told me that Ma was up at
the house.

On the walls by the tables there were blackboards
with Stroh's Beer emblems on them. They were for
writing down all the latest euchre victories
like SHORTY-BENJAMIN-AND-JOHN-RAY-
WEEDIE-SKUNKED-BY-FRED-SHADER-AND-
JUNIOR-SULTS-AUGUST-29, or EWING-JUSTICE-
AND-TUD-WROLSEN-SKUNKED-BY-BILLY-
BARRY-AND-JOE-BOB-WOLVEN-SEPTEMBER 8.
The blackboard up above the table where my father
was   playing   read   LEE-WAYNE-JACKSON-
SKUNKED-BY-JIM-OTIS-CHURCHWARDEN-
SEPTEMBER-26.

The murder had been committed on September
29th.

Ma was still big. Even though I was taller than
she was now, and I guess I weighed more, I wasn't

sure I really believed it. I guess I still felt, when I walked into her kitchen and she turned from the soup pot to hug me, that she could as easily as not just crush me or smother me without even thinking, like some kind of great she-bear from the hills.

Her red hair was thinning, but not graying yet. Her calf muscles bulged out from under the floral print dress that went halfway down them, and the slip that went an inch or so further, as she stood over the stove. Her arms were still massive and powerful, and she still filled the room with her presence as much as her body, and as much as the ham hocks and cornbread and pea soup on the stove filled it with their aroma.

Pa arrived and Louise Ann, my kid sister, and we sat down to supper.

"Will you say grace, Ryland?" Ma asked, looking sharply across the table at me. I knew it wasn't that she cared all that much about grace. It was just one of her ways of trying to make feel uncomfortable about my "city ways."

"Oh, Ma," I said, annoyed and embarrassed. "I . . ."

What was I going to say? That I didn't remember any graces? That I would have felt like some kind of idiot and hypocrite saying one even if I did? None of the above, obviously, even though they were both true. But then Louise Ann broke in with a lightning-fast bit of gibberish about the Lord making us truly grateful, which I was.

Louise Ann was thirteen, my youngest sister, the only one left at home. My two kid brothers were away in the service, and my older sister, Marie, was a beautician in Pittsburgh. Louise Ann was starting to get pretty, as pretty as she had a chance to be in Clove Valley. I wondered if she'd break away when she grew up like Marie and I had, or if she'd just stay around home, marry some guy who'd eventually take over the store and the euchre game from Pa, gain a hundred and fifty pounds real quick, and be stuck here for life. She seemed pretty content with the way things were, so far. All I heard her talk about was boys who came into the store, and gossip about girl friends at school.

Well, she was young yet, and there was still hope for her. I wasn't so different when I was her age. When I was thirteen, I was following Jim Otis Churchwarden all over the place, thinking I wanted to grow up to be just like him and drive hot rods. My sister Marie was sixteen then, and I thought she was the most stuck-up, obnoxious creature I'd ever seen, always putting on airs and acting like the rest of the family—me especially, or so I felt at the time—were no better than dirt for being so common. I can remember Pa saying, one time, "I don't know how anyone so skinny can be so big for her britches." But I changed, too—maybe I did it partly to show up Marie, I don't know. So Louise Ann still had time.

I realized with a start that Louise Ann was the same age as Leona Blye Churchwarden.

I asked Louise Ann if she'd like to come and visit me in Washington.

"When?" she asked, grinning shyly, not committing herself before she'd heard out the offer.

"Oh, what about Thanksgiving?" I said. "I could

take you to see where I work at the Justice Department, and the Washington Monument, and the Capitol Building where Congress works . . ."

"Works? Ha!" my father interjected. "Steals the taxpayers' money, you mean. I don't see why we go to the trouble of electing a President who knows what the country needs, and then send a bunch of crooks and scalawags up there to hamstring him."

There certainly wasn't any point in getting into a political discussion with my father, so I ignored him and asked again: "What about it, Lou Ann? Want to come?"

"Well, I don't know," she said, biting her lower lip. "I hate to miss Thanksgiving dinner at Aunt Dora's. Cousin Stevie Parkins'll be there, and Carolee Blye says he kinda likes me a lot, and . . ."

"Ol' Jim Otis still givin' 'em the slip?" my father asked suddenly, chuckling.

"They'll catch him," I said. And then, with maybe a little too much emphasis, "Don't worry about that."

"I hope they never get him," Pa said, even more emphatically. "Little tramp got what was comin' to her."

I shuddered, but I still wasn't going to be drawn into an argument with Pa. "Well, that's for the law to decide," I said. "And there's not a chance in the world he'll escape. I wouldn't be surprised if they'd got him already."

My father just snorted.

"Just don't seem right at all," said Ma. "Seems like only yesterday that you was runnin' around here in shirttails, thinkin' that Jim Otis was the greatest thing since penny candy. And now you're comin' back down

here in your city suit and your fancy necktie, plannin'
to arrest him."

I still didn't say anything. I just toyed with my soup
silently, hoping that somehow the whole topic would
just pass over and be forgotten. I would have changed
the subject if I could, but I just couldn't think of a
thing to say.

"Is that the way they teach you to eat up there in
Washington, D.C.?" said Ma. "I wonder you stay alive.
Why, I remember when you used to bring Jim Otis
home for dinner, back when you was just a tad and he
was just a-growin' his first mustache, how you and him
could just eat up a storm. And I'd say, 'Now there's a
boy who knows how to appreciate a well-cooked
meal, he surely does.' And then, after supper, he'd
take out his banjo, and just start playin' so pretty it
was like wind blowin' through the valleys, and . . ."

"Oh, that's just not true, Ma!" I burst out. "I only
brought Jim Otis home for dinner two or three, maybe
four times, and he only brought his banjo here once!
He had so many young kids he was busy being a big
shot in front of, he didn't have any more time for me
than that, especially when he found out that Marie
had the good sense not to want to have anything to do
with him!"

"I thought he was cute," said Louise Ann.

"What?" I asked, unbelieving. "You can't mean that!
You're just a baby—you don't know what you're talking about."

I was sputtering now. It seemed more and more urgent, and more and more hopeless, to try to get the
truth of the situation across to these people. "Do you

. . . can you . . . don't you remember what he did?—what he just did three days ago? That . . . that poor little girl he killed—she was no older than you are."

"Well, that proves I'm old enough to think he's cute," said Louise Ann, with a sassy, defiant gleam in her eyes that chilled me.

"That little Leona Blye was a no-account little baggage, anyway," said Ma firmly, as though she had just settled the whole question once and for all.

"That's true," said Louise Ann. "She was always putting on airs back in the sixth grade; thought she was so special. A lot of the girls were glad enough when she didn't come back to school last year, I can tell you that much."

I felt like I'd stepped into a nightmare. I just couldn't comprehend what I was hearing; couldn't put the words together in my mind with the images that were already there. Nothing would mesh at all. They strained and grated and battered against each other, and made my head hurt. I was so frustrated, I was almost ready to break down and cry; and, in fact, I think my voice must have had a strangled sob in it when I finally found it and was able to speak again.

"You don't know what you're talking about!" I said. "Listen to me, I've seen the pictures of what Jim Otis did to that poor girl! It was horrible! It was cruel, it was inhuman, it was sickening! What does it matter what she did in the sixth grade? She was just a child, and he . . . he . . . If you could see those pictures, you'd know."

"Can't put too much stock in lookin' at pictures, Ry," said Ma. "Livin' down here's how you get to know about the people down here, not lookin' at pictures. Now eat your soup. Down here we can't afford to waste food like maybe they can up in Washington, D.C."

CHAPTER 3

Well, there was no question about one thing, anyway: I wasn't going to continue hanging around my parents' house for however long it took the police to track down Jim Otis. I was going to have to put any notions I may have had about a sentimental journey home out of my mind completely—if I had ever had any such notions—and get myself out of Clove Valley altogether, and back into the real world, if I wanted to preserve my sanity at all. I wasn't sure how close I could get to the real world in Passaqua County, but I went over to Waynesville, checked into the Holiday Inn there, and spent the night in my room watching Monday Night Football on TV.

Waynesville was an industrial town, a factory town, fairly large but not too exciting, and Monday Night Football was about the summit of what I figured I could expect from it. The next day, I reported in to Captain Falkner. He told me they still had no lead on Jim Otis, but they were still sure he was in the area, and they would be picking him up anytime now, I could count on it. They had the bus station staked out and roadblocks set up on every road leading out of the county. There was no way that he could get far.

I didn't know about that. It wasn't that I had any particular respect for Jim Otis Churchwarden as a human being, but there were some things I believed I did know about him, and that I had to give him credit for. And right up at the top of the list was that he knew the hills, and the woods, and the back roads of Passaqua County, and all the mountains and valleys around it, so well that he could walk out of the county in broad daylight, stark naked, in any one of a dozen different directions without the state police ever laying eyes on him. So I wasn't about to make a dentist appointment in Washington for the day after tomorrow on the strength of Captain Falkner's assurances. But as long as I didn't have any new orders from the home office, I supposed I was still on the case, if you could call what I was doing being on the case. I made plans to stay at the Holiday Inn a while longer and wait for the real cops to wrap it up.

I spent the afternoon in my room typing up my progress report, which was short but in triplicate. Then I shined my shoes, and watched some daytime TV. There was nothing on that was likely to give old Howard Cosell much of a run for his money, but it did contribute toward driving me pretty stir-crazy by the end of the afternoon. When Tuesday evening came around, I was really in the mood for some action, although I didn't expect to find much of anything around Waynesville.

I went over to the Holiday Inn restaurant for supper, and there was one young chick there waiting on tables who wasn't bad—at least, she didn't look like a hillbilly. She was medium-tall and very slender, with small, hard, erect-looking breasts and a nice ass that her uniform fit tight across. Her face was just a little bit chubbier than her body, with full, pouting, very crimson lips, and eyes that were kind of selfish and kind of sexy.

I made sure I sat at one of her tables, and started making my pitch. There was something about her personality that turned me off, but I didn't let that bother me too much—what the hell, you don't have to like somebody for a one-night stand in a strange town. In a way, that makes it more exciting.

"What time do you get off?" I asked her.

"Eleven o'clock," she said. "But that doesn't mean I don't already have plans for after."

"Do you?"

"Do I what?"

"Have plans for after."

"That's for me to know and you to find out."

She put her nose in the air, turned on her heel, and walked off. But I noticed that her hips were wiggling just a touch more than they had been before.

"Say, what happens in this town after eleven?" I asked the next time she passed by.

"Nothing. Nothing ever happens in this town."

"Then what does an exciting girl like yourself do for excitement?"

"I look at myself in the mirror. *And* I always make sure to stay away from strange guys who try to pick me up, because they always turn out to be such a drag."

I left a tip that was generous enough to give her the impression that I was a real generous guy, without being so large as to give her the impression that I thought she was a hooker. Then I brought my car around to the side of the restaurant and waited till eleven for her to come out.

She looked even better out of her waitress' uniform. She was arrow-slim but sexy in her slacks and tight sweater and push-up bra. She was chewing gum, and she pretended not to notice me, but she walked by near enough to where I was parked for me to call out to her.

"Hi," I said.

"Oh. It's you." Her voice was cold as ice, but all the signals were still go.

"Hop in," I said. "We'll go see the sights."

"I've got my own car."

"OK, we'll take yours," I said, getting out from behind the wheel of mine.

She regarded me like something that had crawled out from under a rock.

"You drive," she said.

We went to a place that drew most of its crowd from the community college, and had music from a rock band made up of four kids with long hair that was still short enough that they could grease it down and look respectable on the streets when they weren't playing rock and roll. They didn't have much talent, but they played loud enough and more or less on the beat.

That was all we really needed for our purposes, which were to work up a sweat, get a little turned on, give each other a preliminary display of how our bodies moved. The music was much too loud to talk over, which was all to the good, because I doubted that we'd have much to say to each other anyway, after we'd exchanged names. (Hers was Edna, and her body moved just fine, for someone in my frame of mind: it moved like she wanted to get laid.)

I was becoming more and more locked into the conclusion that I didn't like her very much at all. And she seemed to have settled pretty definitely into the attitude of contempt for me—or maybe it was just a generalized contempt for the male sex—that she had started out with. We were thrown together by boredom and horniness, and held together by the realization that neither of us was going to do any better for that evening. And horniness.

What was it about her that I disliked so much? I didn't know, exactly, and I didn't want to think about it a whole lot, either—I was out to have a good time, after all. You know, her attitude, I would have answered if pressed. It's just kind of snotty, it's like, you know, her . . . attitude.

"I've got a bottle of Jack Daniel's in my room at the motel—we could stop by for a nightcap," I said.

"Nah, I don't want to hang around that Holiday Inn—too many dumb-assed jerks there. Besides, I got my job to think of. You can come up to my place for a couple of minutes if you want."

We went up to a small, clean, ugly efficiency apartment. I didn't waste any time—why bother? As soon as we stepped in the door I grabbed her and kissed her.

She kissed back. She had a small, narrow tongue that flicked in and out of my mouth like a snake's.

It was a case of making up in quantity for what was lacking in quality. We made love once, then twice, very quickly. I had the feeling that I'd have to get it up again real fast, or she wouldn't let me hang around; so I did. I was on top both times. She thrashed around a whole lot, I'll say that much for her—she really moved around like crazy. She came the first time but not the second, which I thought was a bit unusual.

I was trying to get her to go down on me, sort of pushing down on her head and working my body up, and I think she was just about starting to get the idea, when there was a loud knocking on the door.

She got up, pulled on a floor-length robe with fuzzy hem and cuffs, and went out to answer the door. I heard her voice and another that sounded very drunk and very young, in angry, urgent conversation.

"What are you doing here at this hour? Go home."

"I can't, Sis. I gotta come in. I'm in trouble."

"I don't care. You're drunk. You go home. You can't—"

"I gotta come in!"

The boy pushed past her and ran into the room. Then he saw me, and stopped short.

For a moment a whole new level of consternation was added to the fear he had come in with. He looked back toward the door, then over toward his sister, then back at me.

Finally, a broad, impish grin spread over his face. It

was a real kid-brother grin, full of malicious delight, and I could see the reaction in Edna.

"Hey-y-y-y-y, Sis!" he crowed. "Oh-ho-o-o-o!"

"Thank you," said Edna icily. "Now, if you're quite finished, it's very late and I'd like some privacy in my own apartment, so will you please be good enough to leave this instant."

"Sorry, Sis, I can't," he slurred, lurching past her again as she stood between him and the kitchenette. "I'm in trouble. I gotta have a place to hide out for a couple o' days, while I think things over."

He opened the refrigerator and swayed in front of it, squinting with disapproval at the contents. I decided I might as well get up and get dressed. At this stage of the game, it didn't look like there was much more chance of my getting any blow job that night.

"Well, you're certainly not going to hide out here," Edna said. "I never heard of such a nerve! I want you to close my refrigerator door and get out of my life, and do it fast. I've got better things to do with my life' than take care of every worthless drunken young juvenile delinquent who runs in here. You got yourself into trouble, you can get yourself out."

All of a sudden it hit me what it was that made me dislike her so much. She was Marie, my older sister, right down to a *T*. Marie, exactly. Every snotty attitude, every supercilious gesture. Sure—that was why I could relate to her in the first place, why she didn't seem like she belonged down here with the rest of the hillbillies either. And it was also why her personality grated on me so much.

"Wha' d'ya mean, every worthless . . . I'm your

brother!" began the kid, but he saw the impassive glare on Edna's face and realized it was useless to continue on that tack.

"Better things to do, huh?" he said, facing her with hands on hips, sassing her. "Yeah, I can see that. But the way I figure it, if you ain't already done it, he ain't worth doin' it with, anyway."

"You get out of here right this instant!" she hissed, making a grab for him. But he danced out of her reach.

He was about sixteen, and he looked like he might have stepped out of a James Dean movie—or like one of the young kids who might hang around someone like Jim Otis Churchwarden. But I felt an instinctive kinship with him in spite of all that, and in spite of myself. He was like me with Marie. He was cocky, but I could sense beneath the cockiness an uncertain, disconcerting fear that maybe she really was as superior to him as she acted like she was. The tension between them was starting to excite me in a strange way. I found myself rooting for the kid to hold his own with her.

"What kind of trouble are you in?" I asked him.

"Oh, well, it ain't nothin' much, really—I just wanted to stay outa the way for a couple o' days, you know, gi' me a chance to think things over an' decide what to do. I was out drivin' in my folks' car—I just borrowed it, you know, hot-wired it an' borrowed it, an' I kinda sideswiped this other car. Nobody was hurt, or nothin', but I'd, you know, I'd had a couple o' drinks, and I just figured I'd better take off runnin' before the cops got there, an' . . ."

"Why, you good-for-nothing little runt!" She snarled at him, still keeping her voice down so as not to make a scene that the neighbors would hear—nothing that would cause talk, not for Edna. "I ought to call the police and turn you in myself. Maybe that would knock some decency and respect into you—God knows nothing else has."

"Look, if you won't let me stay, how 'bout at least givin' me a ride across town?" he asked, a faltering note creeping into his voice. "I've got some friends over there, an' I know they'll let me stay with them, but it's too far to walk, an' if I start wanderin' around the streets at this hour, the cops . . ."

Edna just tossed her head disdainfully and pointed at the door. I felt something well up inside me, and before I knew it I heard myself saying:

"Hell, I'd give you a ride, except my car's over at the Holiday Inn."

I don't know whether I meant it, or whether I just figured I was safe in making the offer because I knew I couldn't follow through on it, and it just seemed like a good way of baiting Edna.

If that was what I was doing, it worked. She gave me a look of pure loathing, and I felt a thrill that I hadn't anywhere near gotten from making love to her.

"Holiday Inn? That's not far from here," the kid said. "It's only a couple of minutes' walk, an' I know a back way we can get there without being seen."

I left with him. I felt like I must have taken leave of my senses—after all, even though this had nothing to do with my jurisdiction, I was still a cop, of sorts, and how was I going to explain it if I got caught running through a back alley with this hit-and-run-driving, car-stealing juvenile delinquent?

But on the other hand, I couldn't very well stay at Edna's any longer, that was for sure. I'd seen to that. And in a crazy way, I felt a tremendous rush as I ducked through backyards and alleys and behind a shopping center with this young fugitive. It was the most exciting thing I'd done since—well, since I was a kid, following around after Jim Otis. Could that really be true?

Edna's face had been white and bloodless as we left, her hands balled into little fists. It was hard to tell which of us she loathed more intensely at that moment, but her parting words were directed at me.

"Once a red-neck, always a red-neck," she had spat out at me.

We slipped in through the back of the Holiday Inn parking lot and picked up my car. He gave me directions as we drove across town, but beyond that we didn't talk much. He'd been pretty alert while we were cutting through the back alleys, but now he seemed to be getting a lot drunker again; and the excitement I'd felt as we ran out of Edna's was starting to wear pretty thin. I was beginning to think about who I was, and to ask myself the questions I'd glossed over before about just what the hell I thought I was doing.

In his drunken way, though, he seemed to feel like we were still real buddies. We arrived at our destination, a darkened, drab-looking bungalow in a street full of identical bungalows, on the outskirts of town near the factory. I pulled up in front of it, and he slid out, but leaned back in the door and peered at me.

"Coming in?" he asked.

"No," I said. "I've got to get back to . . ."

"Ah, come on," he said. "Come on in an' meet my friend. She's a really far out chick. Much nicer than my sister."

"Oh, look . . ." I really wanted to go. The fun had gone out of it for me, and I didn't want to meet any of his friends. But I found myself getting out of the car and going up the front walk with him; I don't know why. I just couldn't override his drunken insistence, I guess; and I guess it just seemed to me like I was part of someone else's night, and the night wasn't quite over yet.

The kid knocked on the door several times with what appeared to be a code knock—three shorts and a long, repeated over and over. On about the fourth repeat, the door was opened by a young girl.

She was wearing a faded men's bathrobe and had a pleasant fleshy face that might have been fogged with sleep or might always have looked that way. She welcomed us in with a nod, and went over to put coffee on the stove. We sat down at the kitchen table.

"That's Carolee," the kid said.

"I'm Ry," I said. "Are your parents away?"

"I live here by myself," she said. "I work at the factory."

I couldn't believe it. "But you don't look more than fifteen," I said.

She shrugged. "They don't care how old I am, long

as I give 'em a day's work," she said. "Nobody ever asked me."

"Carolee moved into town about two, three months ago," the kid said, with obvious admiration in his voice. "She can take care of herself real good. She's got her old man staying with her now. He's . . ."

"He's not my old man," said Carolee from over by the stove. She glared at the kid with extreme annoyance, but he didn't seem to notice. He just went on, drunk and talkative, the words tumbling out of him, and the admiration in his voice even more pronounced.

"Well, even if he ain't, he's still some kind o' fantastic guy," the kid said. "You oughta meet him, if he wasn't asleep—hey! Maybe you oughta stay here overnight, too, and you can meet him in the morning."

I shook my head no.

"If you don't quiet down and *shut up*, everyone on the block'll be wakin' up," said Carolee.

He lowered his voice to a loud whisper, but within ten words it was back up to the level it had been at.

"Anyway, he's got this chopper—Harley—that he cut down an' rebuilt himself, customized it an' painted it an' everything. Purple an' black, with gold speckles. An' he can ride that mother—I saw him jump over two cars with it once, just like Evel Knievel."

Carolee shoved a large mug of steaming hot coffee in front of him, glaring at him with a fierce look. She gave me a cup, too, but she still didn't sit down with us at the table. She put the coffeepot back on the stove top and stood over near it. She had moved so silently it was as if she had never left her post by the stove, but her presence and the message she had flashed the kid were unmistakable.

He seemed to have missed the point, however. He went right on talking.

"Yeah, he's somethin' else. He could be better than Evel Knievel, if he wanted to. Or if he wanted to drive cars for money, he could be better'n Richard Petty or A. J. Foyt or any o' those guys. But he don't do none o' that big-shot shit, hell, no. He's just one o' the boys, he ain't gonna let bein' no big shit go to his head, no, sir."

The kid paused for a sip of coffee, then leaned over the table to me, a dreamy, drunken, self-important smirk on his lips.

"Matter o' fact, he's on the lam right now, jus' like us."

"Some people talk too damn *much!*" snapped Carolee, with an emphasis that sprang from someplace deep inside that seemed to surprise even her. The kid shook his head a few times, as if he'd been slapped. Then the smirk came back, and a little giggle, and he said:

"Don't worry, Carolee. This guy's OK. He helped me out. He's my buddy."

"What did this fellow do?" I asked.

The kid puffed up to another notch of self-importance.

"He kilt Carolee's sister."

"Wait a second." I was seized by a sudden chill; I felt as though the walls of the room were contracting around me. "You mean he's . . ."

"Jim Otis Churchwarden," said the kid. "You know him?"

"Sure he does," said a booming, mocking voice behind me. "Hey, there, little Cousin Ry! Understand you come all the way back home from Washington, D.C., just to see me, hey? Well, now, if that don't beat all with a green hickory stick, hey, Carolee?"

CHAPTER 4

All the energy in that room came together with such sudden and jarring force that even the teen-ager felt it. He became suddenly quiet, his hands sliding off the table into his lap and his body hunching over, head downward.

I couldn't turn around. I felt that I should have. I told myself, in a dreamlike but crystal-clear series of commands, that I should whirl immediately, reflexively, toward the voice. And as I turned, I should already have calculated from the sound of his voice how far he was from me, and I should instinctively have gauged how long it would take me to roll out of my chair, and how many steps I would need to get across the floor to him. My head would have swiveled around, leading my body, and I would have determined with my peripheral vision whether or not he had a gun, in time to decide whether or not I should go for it, before I committed myself to leaving my chair. Then, having made the decision to go for it, I should have decided exactly what evasive action I would need to take, and I should have taken it.

Instead, I stared straight ahead of me, immobilized

for the first interminable moment by panic, and then by the rush of thoughts about what I should be doing. They washed over me again and again, like an endless series of waves, pounding me until my eyes glazed and I felt faint. All I could do was tense every muscle in my body, hold on tight, stare straight forward, and fight to stay conscious.

When my brain was able to focus on anything, I became intensely aware of Carolee. I could see her out of the corner of my eye. She still said nothing, betrayed not a flicker of emotion; but I thought I sensed some sort of difference in her.

What the difference was, it was hard to say. She didn't appear to feel threatened by me, not at all. For that matter, she didn't look as though she expected to be rescued by me, either. But her eyes were on me, and they didn't leave me, even though I couldn't bring myself to look at her.

All of a sudden Jim Otis was sitting down at the table across from me. He had moved across the room so silently, it was as though he had just materialized there in the space of a heartbeat, or as if he had always been sitting there, grinning at me, and I had just not been aware of him until that moment.

Jim Otis was tall and lithe, with a spontaneous but conscious grace to his movements that made everything he did seem just that much out of the ordinary. He was unshaven now, his hair rumpled, tufts of his mustache sticking this way and that, but none of that served to make him any less striking a figure than I remembered him, and certainly none of it made him any the less in command of the situation. He was wearing an old pair of jeans, and a red-and-black checked flannel hunting jacket, with no shirt under it.

Was there a gun in the pocket of that jacket? I had the idea I'd seen a bulge on one side as he sat down—a very strong feeling that on some subliminal level I'd seen it; but of course everything had happened so quickly that I hadn't really been able to see anything very clearly. And now his pocket was below the level of the table.

"Well, now, what d'ye got to say for yourself, kid?" he asked me, his eyes twinkling with a kind of mocking benevolence.

I didn't say anything.

"Hey, come on, kid, cat got your tongue? You don't have to feel no call to be no kinda bashful around your ol' cuz, Cousin Ry. What d'ye got to say for yourself, come all the way down from Washington, D.C., to visit? What's the good word?"

"I . . . didn't expect to see you here," I stammered.

"Hey, now, I'll just bet you didn't! You-all did come down 'specially to see ol' Jim Otis, though, didn't you now there, honey brother?"

He didn't even have to snap off the question at the end—the effect was the same. I knew he expected a direct answer, and I was going to have to dance to his tune.

I tried nodding my head, but his smile only broadened, and I knew that meant a nod wasn't enough. I'd never seen a smile stay on one person's face for so long and still look sunny and bright and unstrained—especially considering the menace that I sensed behind it.

"How . . . how'd you know that, Jim Otis?" I asked.

"Ah, shucks, ain't no secrets down around this part of the country, you know how gossip does git around," he said. "Well, now, if that don't just beat all to hell. All the way back from Washington, D.C., to Passaqua County, just to see me—my little baby cousin, who went off to the big city and made such a success for hisself as a big ol' cop."

His voice didn't even lose its warmth and good humor on the last word, but its effect wasn't lost on the kid. He reacted with a sudden spasm of shock, spilling the coffee from the cup he held in his hand all over his lap. It was still steaming hot, and it must have burned like hell, but he didn't make a sound.

"Hey, Carolee, what're you doin' to these poor ol' boys here—trying to get 'em sobered up?" Jim Otis said. "How 'bout gettin' us each a beer?"

Silently, the girl complied, bringing three bottles of Stroh's and three glasses over to the table.

"Hey, ain'tcha gonna pour for Cousin Ry, Carolee? That ain't no way to treat a guest, now."

She poured beer into my glass, still without uttering a word or betraying an emotion. I started to lift my hand to stop her, but I realized that of course it would be the wrong thing to do. I didn't drink the beer.

Jim Otis poured himself a glass, then leaned forward across the table toward me, addressing me in a cozy, confidential manner.

"Now, answer me this, though, Cousin Ry," he said. "Ain't this a hell of a nicer way for a couple of old boys to get together for a fam'ly reunion than if'n I had to wear a pair o' handcuffs an' you had to tote a big ol' gun an' go flashin' a badge all over the place at everybody?"

"Sure is, Jim Otis," I said.

I wasn't forgetting my responsibility, not for a second. First I had to determine for sure whether or not he had a gun. I thought he did—it certainly seemed as if he did—but I couldn't be positive. It seemed as though he had to have one, even though I hadn't actually seen it. He wouldn't be so careless as to let himself get caught without one.

Not like me.

But then, I wasn't the fugitive—he was. I wasn't even supposed to be chasing him. When they caught him and gave him to me, that was when I was supposed to show up with my gun and handcuffs.

Besides, this was Jim Otis Churchwarden. I naturally expected him to be a step ahead of me, like he always had been.

But I wasn't giving up. I'd just bide my time and wait for an opening.

"Yessiree, we couldn't hardly jest set back an' talk about ol' times, what with you takin' me on that train back to Ohio in handcuffs, now could we?" said Jim Otis. "Be no way in the world, you settin' up straight an' stiff, tryin' not to scare the other passengers by lettin' on they had a dangerous felon in their midst. An' then there'd be another cop along, too, so's I couldn't bang you-all on the head with my handcuffs an' make my excape by divin' outa the window o' the train, so you couldn't do nothin' to let on to him that you was ol' good buddies an' kinfolk to that murderin'

man on t'other side o' the law, could you now? Yessir,
I sure am glad I happen to run into you here in Carolee's kitchen like this, so's we could set down an' have
a beer together, talk over ol' times an' kind o' get ac-
quainted all over again, 'fore I have to go up an' turn
myself in."

Now it was my turn to almost knock over my glass.
"What?" I said.

His eyes twinkled again. Was he being straight
with me? I searched his eyes as best I could, but I
couldn't find a clue.

"Yup, I been a-thinkin' about it, these last couple o'
days. Reckon I'll jest have to go ahead an' do 'er
pretty quick. No fun hidin' out, jest a-runnin' away
from good buddies like ol' Cousin Ry the rest o' my
life, now, is there?"

He studied the foam at the bottom of his glass.

"What d'ye suppose they'll give me, Cousin? How
long d'ye suppose they'll keep ol' Jim Otis locked up
behind them bars?"

I looked across the table at Jim Otis. I had a sudden, heartstopping flashback to my youth, and the
idea of my cousin actually behind bars became terri-
bly real, and hit me with the force of a high voltage
electric shock.

"Reckon it depends on what they charge me with,
don't it? First degree, second degree, manslaughter—
guess it depends on whether ol' judge has a soft spot
in his heart for ol' Jim Otis. Mebbe if I can make him
smile once or twice . . . Play him a song, hey? I ain't
gonna be able to get me no big-city lawyer—don't figger I can get away with pleadin' self-defense, do ye?"

He gave me a rueful look. Now I could get back to my role and feel like a cop again, magnanimous and understanding but still realistic, stern, and unyielding.

"I don't think there's much of a chance of that, Jim Otis," I said. "But . . ."

Jim Otis leaned back in his chair; put his feet up on the table. "Well, it don't make no nevermind," he said. "I ain't blamin' you for nothin'. Matter o' fact, mebbe some good'll come out o' this. Leastways, now you can be the one as takes me in. Be quite a feather in your cap, hey, up-and-comin' young G-man like yourself?"

"I guess so," I said. "But look, Jim Otis, it's just my job. I don't like to . . ."

He seemed to be growing older and more benevolent, almost grandfatherly, with every word he spoke. I found myself picturing him in prison, growing old, his young manhood and the prime of his life fading away from him. I felt uncomfortable as hell.

Then, as quickly as he had conjured up the mood, he broke it. His broad grin returned, and he whooped and slapped his thigh.

"Hey, I'll tell you what," he said. "Why don't the three of us have a little fun first?"

"The three of us?" I repeated, confused. I glanced over at the kid, who was trying to make himself look as small as possible over on his side of the table.

"You, me, and Carolee," said Jim Otis. The kid looked relieved, but went on crouching and concentrating on trying to make himself look inconspicuous. "We oughta make this a celebration! It ain't every day my favorite baby cousin come back home from the big city, to send ol' Jim Otis off to the gallows an' make hisself a big name for hisself as a G-man! We can't jest go ahead an' do 'er an' have 'er all over an' done with, without we have us a little party first. Sure won't be able to go an' have us no party afterwards, now, will we?"

"But we can't . . ." I began.

"Tell you what we'll do," he said. "You know, I've got me a little shack up in the mountains as don't nobody know about, not even the revenooers, an' I got my finest still right up there. Yup, an' I got some vittles packed up there, an' we can have ourselves one hell of a party, 'fore you have to go an' take me in."

I shook my head; set my face in an official-looking frown. "I'm afraid not, Jim Otis," I said. "I couldn't allow it. But look here, don't feel so pessimistic. I don't think they'll send you to the—"

"Hey! Sergeant Preston! This case is closed!" Whooped Jim Otis, pounding his feet on the table. "Hey, come on now, Cousin Ry, you ain't gonna be no party-pooper on us now, are you?" His voice sounded as jovial and comradely as ever.

I rememberd again that he might have a gun. If he did, I didn't think I could get to him in time to disarm him, not with the table between us, not even if I kicked the table over on him. I tried to remember what they'd told us about a man with a gun with a table between you, but nothing seemed exactly to fit this situation. If he didn't have a gun, I might be able to take him. He was bigger than I was, but I'd had a lot of training. Of course, I'd never actually had to apply any of it in the field before, but the principle was certainly the same.

I'd never had to try to take on Jim Otis before, either.

But despite whatever feelings I might have had as a kid growing up, I reminded myself, there was nothing invincible about Jim Otis Churchwarden.

He just seemed so damn sure of himself. He must have a gun.

"We jest gonna get ready an' go, right now. Hey, we gonna have a good ol' time, ain't we now, Cousin Ry?"

He got up from the table and went into the bathroom, and I heard the sound of running water. If I was going to make a move, this looked like it had to be the time.

I wondered if he had meant it about turning himself in after we went up in the hills together.

From everything I remembered about him when he was my idol as a kid, he always kept his word.

But as a law enforcement officer, I couldn't see myself voluntarily agreeing to a proposition like that. It was out of the question.

I couldn't guess what Carolee's response would be if I tried to surprise Jim Otis in the bathroom. Maybe she'd try to warn him and protect him, but on the other hand maybe she was just a prisoner, too, like I was. Then again, maybe she'd just go on standing by the stove, silent and sphinxlike, no matter what happened.

"Are you . . . really Leona's sister?" I asked.

She nodded.

"Older sister?"

She nodded again. "I'm fifteen," she said.

She had a low voice, a sort of a sweet voice. Not sweet as a theatrical effect, like it always half seemed Jim Otis' was; and certainly the sweetness wasn't directed at me. It was just the quality that her voice had.

I leaned toward her and spoke in hushed tones, almost a whisper, although the shower was still running in the bathroom and would easily have drowned out any sounds from where we were.

"Is Jim Otis holding you as a hostage here, or are you hiding him out?"

She turned back away from me, to face the stove.

Jim Otis called from the bathroom, "Hey, Carolee, go in an' pack a bag. An' put a couple extra pairs o' clean socks in for Cousin Ry."

She went into the bedroom. I waited a few moments longer, then started very slowly and quietly toward the bathroom door.

The kid watched me in frightened silence. I gave him what I hoped was a reassuring glance, then remembered with a jolt that it was me he was frightened of, not Jim Otis. That didn't seem right. It was Jim Otis who was the murderer, not me. I forced the picture of the two bodies in front of my eyes again, to remind myself. I tiptoed halfway across the room, and then the water stopped.

I froze. Jim Otis came breezing out the bathroom door, naked now except for the hunting jacket, which he had slipped back into.

That seemed strange, too. It would feel itchy against his skin, after a shower. I strained to see if I could tell anything from the shape of his pocket. I wondered if it was really the gun I was afraid of.

"Yeah, you-all can use the bathroom now, Cousin Ry," said Jim Otis, as friendly as ever. If he had any suspicion that I was stalking him, he disguised it so perfectly that I was convinced he knew exactly what I was doing. "He'p yourself to my razor if'n you want, but keep your cotton-pickin' hands offen my tooth-brush."

Within fifteen minutes, we were packed and ready to go. Jim Otis wore a fresh pair of jeans now, a faded denim work shirt, and hiking boots. He had on a cowboy hat, too, and that same hunting jacket. He carried his banjo in his left hand, and Carolee brought out a couple of small backpacks. She was wearing jeans and hiking boots, too, a schoolgirl's white blouse, and a short denim jacket. It was the first light of dawn now, and as they threw the suitcase in the back of my car they looked like a cowboy and his daughter setting out for the Cheyenne rodeo.

Except that she wasn't his daughter, she was his sister-in-law. The big sister to the little girl he'd married and killed in cold blood.

We left the teenage boy in the kitchen. I tried to wigwag some eyebrow signals and facial contortions to him about sending someone to rescue me, but I knew it was no use. He wasn't even looking at me.

"Listen, they're going to miss me at the Holiday Inn," I said. "They'll notice that I'm gone, and then they'll come after you."

Jim Otis threw back his head and laughed. Carolee remained impassive.

CHAPTER 5

I drove. Carolee sat in the front seat beside me. My knees were jammed up under the dashboard and my body jackknifed over the steering wheel, as the front seats had been pushed forward all the way to accommodate Jim Otis' long frame in the back seat of a tiny Gremlin that had never been designed to accommodate more than a small child back there—unless you had a midget doing the driving. He had made room for himself, though, and sat spread out comfortably, his long body draped all the way across the back of the car. He played the banjo as we headed eastward out of town, into the mountains and a hazy sunrise.

The banjo rhythms hammered and rolled, the melodies rose and fell and whined with a droning insistence as we left the dirty factory streets behind.

With Jim Otis drawling out directions from the back, we headed down a country road through scarred, ugly strip-mined hills, then past them and into backwoods farm country, down dirt roads leading off dirt roads, through blue-green rocky fields, and past trailers and ancient farmhouses that came first in clusters, then sparse and more isolated.

I felt like something out of Bonnie and Clyde.

And I couldn't stand it. It left me with an overwhelming sense of embarrassment and humiliation. It was all out of proportion, I suppose, but I couldn't help feeling it, and I couldn't help feeling totally unmanned by it. It was one thing to be kidnapped and held hostage by an armed, or probably armed, escaped murderer—it was frightening, sure. It was a tense and dangerous, possibly lethal situation, but that was part of my job. It went with the badge, as they said; it was one of the risks I'd agreed to undertake when I became a marshal. But to have your abductor insist on calling you "Cousin" all the time, to have a fifteen-year-old girl along for the ride, and finally, to have the whole thing staged to the accompaniment of hillbilly music—it turned everything into a farce. It wasn't fair.

It wasn't fair. Because while it might be a farce, a clown show, a backwoods hayseed mockery of everything I was trying to do in my life, it was still deadly serious for all that: it was a matter of life or death, and having it turned ridiculous by some joker with a banjo didn't change that. Not when he was also an unpredictable, demented killer, who was capable of Lord knew what kinds of atrocities. I remembered the photographs.

"Can't put much stock in lookin' at pictures, Ry. Livin' down here's how you get to know the people down here, not lookin' at pictures."

We passed a dingy blue-and-silver trailer on cement

blocks, with a wisp of smoke coming from a hooded chimney pipe above the roof. There were two small shacks behind it, and some scrawny chickens in the front yard. It was the first house I remembered having seen in about five minutes. There were mostly woods now, on both sides of the road.

> *"Oh, the cuckoo,*
> *She's a pretty bird,*
> *And she warbles*
> *As she flies,*
> *She don't never*
> *Holler cuckoo*
> *Till the Fourth day*
> *Of July,"*

sang Jim Otis.

There weren't going to be any state troopers blocking this road. There probably wasn't anyone on the force who had ever heard of it. A deputy sheriff might pass down it once a month, if that. And even if one did go by us, he wasn't likely to stop and ask some city feller in a cute little citified car if he knew anything about an escaped fugitive named Jim Otis Churchwarden. Especially not some guy out for a drive in the mountains with his daughter—well, she wasn't really young enough to be my daughter; or, at least, I wasn't old enough to be her father.

My . . . what? Sister, I guessed. Come to think of it, I had a sister just about her age; two years younger, in fact. Her sister Leona's age. *"My cousin*

Leona, you remember, don't you, Ry? Of course you do."

I was beginning to wonder if anyone else on this joyride did. Or were we just the typical all-American family out for a little picnicking and banjo-picking up in the mountains?

After which, good old Cousin Jim Otis would turn himself in. Was I being petty, too much of a stickler for law and order to think there was anything wrong with that?

My cousin Carolee, sitting beside me. Would she call me Cousin Ry, too? So far, she didn't call me anything.

I turned around to look at her.

She became aware of my eyes on her, and swiveled her head around to return my gaze just as I had to look back at the road, so I only caught her glance out of the corner of my eye; and when I looked back over she was staring straight ahead once more, and would not look in my direction again.

I didn't feel there was any hostility in her placid ignoring of me. It was just . . . I didn't know. Maybe it was dumb. Another dumb hillbilly, another semi-moronic country cow just waiting her turn to be a child bride and settle down to keep house for the next sixty years, with never a thought in her head.

If she was luckier than her sister.

What was Jim Otis doing with her, anyway? Wasn't one sister enough for him? How much of a monstrous, insane, murderous traveling salesman joke had I gotten myself in the middle of?

"*Walk me down to the station*
With my suitcase in my hand,
And it's fare thee well, my own little lovē,
I'm bound for a far distant land."

Carolee had plump hands, with stubby fingers that played over and under and around each other, that were laced and unlaced endlessly and traced circles across her thigh and around her kneecap. They were in marked contrast to the relaxed placidity of the rest of her body. Her hair was an ash blonde that might still go darker before she grew up. It seemed to have been given a permanent about six months before, so that it was now limp and almost all grown out. It was part stringy and part frizzy, and a few wisps of it fell down into her face. That sounds pretty ugly, but it wasn't ugly, just . . . not what I would have called nice-looking, not my style. Her face, too, sort of broad, with a broad, flat nose, all gently curving, rolling planes, no really sharply etched features. Her mouth just seemed like part of her face, broad and pleasant enough, but not strongly defined, like a real mouth. Not my type—well, she was just a kid, but she wasn't going to grow up to be my type.

I wondered what Eddie, or any of my pals from Washington, would have said about her. Well, I knew: they would have taken one look at her tits and whooped.

She did have nice tits, there was no question about that—big and soft and round, but very firm and shapely. Well, of course they'd be firm: she was so young. Eddie was always kidding around about high school girls, like when we'd be driving and we'd pass a couple of them on the street, walking home from school or just hanging out. He had a song he'd sing, too, as we drove past: *"Hey, little schoolgirl, are you going my way? Let me carry your books home, baby, feel so good today."*

I used to laugh with him, but I never really thought it was all that funny. That was because I was too close to it, on account of people like Jim Otis Churchwarden.

"Turn here," commanded Jim Otis from the back. Another narrow, rutted, rocky dirt road; my rented car would never be the same again. I wondered if the government had any sort of insurance that would cover the repairs for it, or at least if I could put it on my expense account. I hoped I wouldn't have to pay for it myself—I'd end up spending more than my salary, expenses, and per diem all put together, by the time I got finished with this job. I didn't have any idea what department policy was for a situation like this.

I hated not knowing details like that. It really made me feel like a dumb rookie.

". . . Omie, little Omie, you've guessed about right, For I dug on your grave the best part of last night."

"This is where we get out an' walk, ol' Cousin," said Jim Otis, finishing the song with a flourish.

It appeared that he was right. The road had already been enough to knock your teeth out for the last several miles, but up ahead there seemed to be nothing that could be called a road at all.

I stopped the car in its tracks.

"Better pull 'er over, just a trace, there, Cousin," said Jim Otis.

"Why? Afraid someone might want to drive on by us?"

"No-o-o-oo, that ain't it exactly, Cousin," he said. "Although there's motor vee-hickles as can drive a good piece further down this road than that cute li'l ol' toy o' yourn. It's just that I'm a-thinkin' we wouldn't want to have no ol' cops—no offense there, Cousin—flyin' over in no helio-copters an' wonderin' what a cute li'l ol' red car is doin' all by itself up in the middle o' the mountains. They might just be so unkind as to send over a party o' their own to come in an' bust up our party 'fore we ever get ready to come back down, an' that wouldn't be no fun, now, would it? So I figger we might just better pull 'er over and park 'er under that big tree over there."

He pointed.

"Are you crazy?" I said. "This is no fucking jeep—I couldn't even get it over there, much less ever get it out again. What are you planning to do about that?" A sudden panic swept me, and my voice rose in pitch. "Or is this the end of the line—is that what you're trying to tell me?"

"Cousin Ry!" Jim Otis sounded genuinely hurt. Then he laughed, slapped me on the back, and said, "Hey! Come on. Don't you be worryin' so much, there, Cousin—let's just get 'er over there now, and we'll figger a way to get 'er out again when the time comes. Hop out, now, and let me give 'er a try."

I wasn't about to argue. Carolee and I both climbed out of the car, and Jim Otis got in the driver's seat.

I was thinking about making a run for it, but I didn't know the terrain and I decided I wouldn't have a chance. Besides, I was uneasy about leaving Carolee alone with Jim Otis, without knowing for sure if she was there of her own free will.

Jim Otis turned the key in the ignition, and revved up the engine until it roared and whined at a level of volume that I had no idea such a small car could produce; I thought for sure the engine would explode or shake itself right out of the car before he ever started it moving.

But then he kicked it into gear, and it shot off over the terrain, careening through the air from one jolt to the next, chewing up bushes and tiny scrub cedars in its path, bouncing over the rocks.

Halfway across the field the roar of the engine suddenly increased to an even more deafening pitch, and I winced with feeling for my poor Gremlin out of its element as it lurched onward, leaving its muffler behind on a rock.

We abandoned it there under the tree, muffler gone completely and two tires ripped to shreds, and started walking. Jim Otis and I each took one of the backpacks, and he carried his banjo.

The way was uphill, but not too steep at first. There was a lot of undergrowth, and some big bushes with brambles that hung out over the path on both sides, which made for some narrow going. There was no particular protocol on the bramblebushes, as near as I could make out. When the path was wide enough,

we walked abreast. When it narrowed and we had to
go single file; sometimes Jim Otis would stand aside
and let me go first, and other times he would just
plunge ahead himself, apparently giving not a thought
in the world to protecting himself against a rear ambush from me.

And all the time he was laughing, talking about
what a good old time we were going to have, yodeling
and singing snatches of old songs.

I didn't believe it. I just wasn't going to buy it. I
refused to believe that it wasn't a trap, that he wasn't
expecting me to try to jump him. And if he was prepared for whatever I might try, then I sure as hell
wasn't going to be fool enough to try anything.

And if he wasn't baiting a trap for me, then it
would have to mean that he really was planning to
give himself up. And maybe he did just want one last
fling, a sentimental reunion with the kid cousin who'd
followed him around back in the old days.

I remembered, not wanting to, a time when I would
have given my right arm to believe that was true. And
if it was true now, I'd feel like the worst kind of heel
if I were to catch him off guard and force him to sur-
render.

But I couldn't get started thinking like that. I had to
remember what my duty was, keep that in the fore-
front of my mind, and wait for my opening.

We came to what had once been a large clearing,
but was long since heavily overgrown with secondary
growth. In the center of it was an old farmhouse— a
large farmhouse, almost a mansion. In fact, there were
thick columns by the front door.

Not much was left of it now. No windows, most of the roof caved in. There was a smaller building butted up beside it—servants' quarters, probably—and there was a large shade tree next to the small building, which had been half uprooted by a past storm. It was still partly rooted in the ground; a few green, leafy limbs attested to that. But it leaned heavily against the small building, with the result that time and nature's constant pressure had set the small building atilt also, and leaning over against the main house—which now, in its turn, was sagging heavily to one side, pillars and all. All three of them, leaning crazily though they did, were still intact: tree, servant's quarters, big house. The outermost growing limbs of the tree bumped the high gables of the big house, and then veered upward.

"What place is this?" I asked.

"This?" said Jim Otis. "Why, the old Thomas place. Crazy ol' rich feller built it up here 'round about nineteen and ten. You never been up here before?"

"No."

"Never even heerd tell about it?"

"Never have."

"Well, now, that just goes to show what happens when you leave the mountains too soon, 'fore you get to take the time and find out about them, learn what they're all about. Never do get a chance to find out what-all is up there, less'n you get lucky and some ol' pal gives you a shot at a second go-round. How bout' you, Carolee? You ever hear tell o' this place before?"

She shook her head.

"Well, now, there's a mighty interestin' story behind it. Want to hear it?"

She shook her again. "It's all fallin' down," she said.

We walked on, through the overgrown estate—rotting fences around old corrals, a few rusting heavy farm implements. We walked past an old grape arbor gone wild, the trellises rotted and crushed under the weight of the vines long grown out of control. Here, where civilization had held sway over the land within memory, it was harder going than we had encountered anywhere before, with the tough high grasses tangling our feet. It was about two o'clock in the afternoon now, and the heat of the sun was taking its toll on us, too, making the going that much harder.

Behind the estate was a swift-running stream, and we walked along beside it, heading upstream. We were heading into a deep gorge, with rocky bluffs on either side, and we passed long stretches of white water.

I couldn't imagine where we were heading. I felt certain that this couldn't be the route that Jim Otis normally took to get to his cabin—it must be a special obstacle course arranged for my benefit.

I was also sure that he must be more tired than he was letting on. He had to be. I was in excellent shape, too, after all. I'd had all my police training with the department, which was plenty rigorous, and I did the Royal Canadian Air Force exercises on top of that. And I knew how beat I was feeling.

Carolee didn't look as though she liked it very much, but she kept going. I got the impression that she was used to keeping on, even with the things she didn't like very much. Perhaps that included most of her life.

Jim Otis still looked as though he were reveling in the adventure. He was bouncing along with that banjo case in his hand—a banjo, on a virtual forced march like this! He was still carrying on as if it were a picnic. Well, if he wasn't going to show any signs of strain, neither was I. I wasn't going to be the first one to call for a rest.

The gorge was narrowing now, and we were walking right down by the stream. It was a good ten degrees cooler down here than it had been out in the heat of the sun, and a refreshing spray from the rapids blew in our faces and made the going easier.

The worst problem for me now was my shoes. They definitely hadn't been made for this kind of overland hiking, and my feet were starting to blister badly.

"Gettin' tuckered?" Jim Otis asked cheerfully.

"Not too much," I said. "How about you?"

"Me, I'm doin' just fine," he said. "It's the mountain gait, keeps you goin' all day. Gotta get used to it, learn not to fight the country and it'll just naturally help you right along. We'll take us a little rest around the next bend."

"Whatever you like," I said. "Carolee probably needs a rest. This is a pretty rugged trek to take a young girl along on."

"I reckon," said Jim Otis.

The wall of the gorge pinched right down to the rapids as it curved around the bend. To get past the spot, we had to climb up on a ledge that was about two feet wide, and maybe three or four feet over the swirling white water.

Around the corner, it widened out again. There was a flat rock about twenty-five or thirty feet long that sloped up out of the water and rose to meet a group of boulders, on the other side of which the path continued again.

Jim Otis led the way. He leaped off the ledge, made a crouching three-point landing on the rock, holding his banjo case in the air, and clambered up to the top.

I followed his lead. Making a flying leap and coming down on the flat rock some twenty-odd feet from the top, I started running up, crouching and keeping my lead hand close to the ground so I could touch it down for balance if I needed support.

The rock was incredibly slippery! Foam and spray from the rapids had made the surface wet and difficult to keep a footing on, especially with my slick-soled city shoes. I skidded as I went forward, my gait becoming more frenzied and scrambling, and the top of the rock getting closer all too slowly. About eight feet from the upper lip of the rock, I hit a patch of algae.

Panicked, I stiffened upright. My arms waved wildly in the air as I tried to maintain my balance, and I careened backward, standing up, down the rock. Jim Otis, above me, turned at my sudden scream, and I saw a wild gleam in his eyes as I went slipping and sliding away from him, down across the broad expanse of rock shelf and straight for the rapids.

I had made a complete 180-degree turn and was facing the water as I came to the end of the rock. I made a wild grab for the ledge I had started from, and caught it with my elbows and forearms. But there was nothing there to get a solid grip on, and I was up to my waist in rushing water.

Carolee was still on the ledge, and she grabbed my arms and held on. But she didn't have anywhere near the strength to pull me up, or even to keep a hold on me for very long. The water churned and swirled around my legs until I no longer could even feel which way they were pointing, even if they had been able to get up the strength to climb against the current.

But there was no strength in them at all. They felt as if they were already lost to me, already swept away.

Carolee's face was up above me, her eyes wide with terror and helplessness and an overwhelming primal expression of loss that joined itself with the relentless onrushing of the waters to make me feel as if I were already gone.

She was crying and shouting something at me, but even though her face was only two feet away from mine, I could hear nothing. I might as well have been two miles away, and her face might as well have been brought up to such close focus by a telephoto lens.

It felt like that. I felt so distant, so removed, as though I were spying on her private emotions from a long way off, in another world.

Carolee looked up to the rocks in desperation for

Jim Otis, her face contorted into an agonized plea for help.

Carolee seemed flat, two-dimensional, slightly distorted—just as if I were seeing her through a telephoto lens. From the corner of my eye, I saw Jim Otis running down the rock, and he seemed to be moving in slow motion: he seemed to stay a moving speck in the periphery of my vision for a long time.

With the terrifying clarity of logic that comes when you have all the time in the world to think, in the instant ahead of oblivion, my mind registered: *There's no place for him to go. There's no room for him on that ledge.*

Then the roaring of the waters was split by a wild scream from Jim Otis, and I saw a blur come in front of me as he leaped into the air, heading for the ledge. I felt Carolee let go of me and was aware that she moved backward, away from me, off the ledge altogether. Then all the strength went out of my arms; my muscles went limp, the river took hold of me and was bearing me away, and for a space of time that I could never begin to estimate, there was nothing but roaring and a long, dark tunnel.

CHAPTER 6

The next sensation I could understand was the pain in my arms—something I could feel over the churning of the waters. Jim Otis was squeezing me just above the elbows, and he was planted solidly on the ledge above me where Carolee had been. He was shouting something into my face, but I couldn't tell what.

It didn't matter. I knew what I was supposed to do.

My knees and my feet were still useless at first against the waters, but when Jim Otis had pulled me a little higher and I was able to hook my chest over the ledge, I started to be able to plant them against the side of the rock, and to scramble and squirm upward with every part of my body. Jim Otis had his arms wrapped under my armpits now, and I was leaving the grip of the rapids. I was going to be all right.

I sat on the ledge, hugging my legs with my arms. "Saved my . . . saved my life," I panted.

"Okay," he said. "Like . . . like I said, be a good time to take a little rest now."

"I'll make it up the rock first," I said stubbornly, still gasping for breath.

"Okay, Cousin, whatever you like," he agreed. "Let Carolee take your pack."

"I'll carry it."

He shrugged.

The sun was going down in the west when we finally came up out of the gorge and arrived at Jim Otis' cabin.

I was so glad to be there that any shelter would have looked good to me, even one that I'd been kidnapped to and almost killed trying to reach. And it was a cozy little cabin at that, no question about it.

Not so little, as a matter of fact—it would do to hold the three of us. It even had two rooms. Both of them were pretty small, but there were two distinct rooms nevertheless. A wall down the middle of the cabin separated a bedroom from the rest of the house, and that led me to assume that Jim Otis had not built the cabin himself. People must have lived up in here in this part of the mountains at one time—this cabin must have belonged to a mountain family long ago, and Jim Otis must have found it and fixed it up— mended the roof, chinked the corners, and made it livable again.

After all, when he came up here he probably stayed for long periods of time to do his moonshining, if only to make the trek up worth his while, so he'd want it to be at least passably comfortable.

I hoped it also meant, since we were going to be stuck here for a while, that he kept it decently stocked with provisions.

Carolee wasn't satisfied to stand around and hope

on that point. From the moment we came in, she had been taking inventory of the place. She was going through the kitchen now, checking out the one kitchen cupboard with its supply of a few canned goods, some dried foods, powdered milk, salt and pepper and coffee and tea, sugar and flour and corn meal.

"Hey, don't worry 'bout none o' that stuff tonight," said Jim Otis. "Let's get us some shut-eye—ol' Cousin Ry can sure use it. We'll go down to the crick for water in the mornin', and you can whip up somethin' then."

"Just lookin' around," she said.

The rest of the kitchen was a counter with a tray that had a few knives and forks and spoons on it, and a pitcher and washbasin. Under it was a wooden box with some old rusty iron pots and pans. There was a mirror over the washbasin that was tarnished in all four corners, but still in one piece and uncracked. In the center of the room was a large wood stove, with a kettle on it. In front of the stove, there was a round table with two chairs by it, each one rickety and wired together with baling wire.

"We can fetch in a box from outside in the mornin'," said Jim Otis apologetically as Carolee inspected the table and chairs. "Never did figger on having two extry people around the table. Never did figger on havin' one, for that matter, if the truth be known; but you always like to keep one extry chair by a table, just in case."

Carolee squinted at the broom in the corner, a

handmade straw one without much straw left to it. She opened up the cedar chest that was the room's only other item of furniture and wrinkled her nose at the smell of camphor, then pawed quickly through the pile of blankets in the box with one hand, while she held the lid open with the other.

Finally she stood, arms folded below her breasts, in the center of the room. She looked up at the rafters and into the corners, scowling at the cobwebs. Then she turned, went into the bedroom, and closed the door.

I waited to see what Jim Otis would do, but if I had expected a dramatic confrontation I was disappointed. Without so much as a second glance in the direction of the closed bedroom doors, he took two steps over to the cedar chest, pulled out a green Army blanket, which he tossed to me, then another one for himself. He knelt down right where he was, unlaced his boots, and slipped them off. He took off his hunting jacket, rolled it up, and put it under his head for a pillow. And if there was a gun in his pocket, then he was sleeping on that, too. He pulled the blanket up over his shoulders, and closed his eyes.

I took off my wet clothes, blew out the lamp, and tried to make myself as comfortable as I could with one inadequate blanket on a cold, rough floor. I fell into an unsettled sleep with the smell of camphor in my nostrils.

Jim Otis and I opened our eyes at almost the same moment, and we rolled over to look at each other.

There was a glint in his eyes that was more than just the sleep glistening in them, and a grin on his lips. He winked at me and slammed the floor with his fist exuberantly.

"Hot damn, Cousin Ry," he said. "Ain't it great to wake up in the mountains, though? Just smell that fresh mountain air."

I was shivering with cold, and every bone and muscle in my body hurt.

He rolled over, got to his feet, and stretched mightily, filling his lungs with the mountain air.

"Makes you feel ready for anything, don't it?"

I got to my feet much more gingerly.

"What did you have in mind?" I asked.

He only grinned again in reply.

Carolee was up already, standing outside the front door, looking across the valley that stretched away beneath us to the hazy blue mountains in the distance.

"How 'bout fixin' us up some breakfast?" Jim Otis asked.

"What do you want?"

"Now, Carolee . . . ah, shoot. Make us up some fried mush."

"Gotta fetch me some water first."

"She doesn't say much, does she?" I said to Jim Otis as we walked down to the stream. There was no need for both of us to go—in fact, it should have been Carolee's job, but for now Jim Otis seemed to want to keep me busy and the two of us together, and he was still calling the shots.

"She's a stubborn one, that Carolee," Jim Otis agreed.

"Seems like she's kind of dumb . . . not all there, maybe."

"Oh, she ain't dumb, no, that ain't it. Ain't sayin' she's no genius, but there ain't nothin' missin' up there. She's just plain stubborn, is all, an' she won't give an inch less'n she's ready in her mind, which runs in its own ways. An' they runs deep."

"That why you're sleeping in the next room?"

"Oho! Hooo-ey!" Jim Otis whooped. "You wouldn't be speculatin' on gettin' a little ol' country gal for yourself, would you, now, Cousin?"

"Not me," I said. "I like my women to be old enough to know what they're doing. I don't mess around with kids."

That just slipped out—I didn't exactly realize the implications until after I'd said it. I didn't want to be the instigator of any gratuitous trouble with Jim Otis. I gave him an apprehensive sidelong glance, but he only chuckled.

We dumped our pails out into the cistern, and went back down to the stream to refill them. On the way back up, Jim Otis asked me:

"Hey, there Cousin Ry, what's them city women like, anyhow?"

"Oh, they're OK," I said.

"No, I want to know," he said. "What's the difference between a city gal an' a li'l ol' country gal? They know some pretty good tricks in the sack? They hotter? Colder?"

"Well, yeah, sure, some of them do, I guess. I've had, you know, some hotter, some colder, you can't—

oh, shit, I don't know! I've never made it with a country girl. I was virgin when I went away to college, if you really have to know."

Jim Otis gave a low whistle. "All the way to college, eh? That why you went away?"

"No, it's not."

"Hey, well, now, you maybe don't know what you're missin', now, do you?" Jim Otis said, musing on the idea. "Could be that's just what you been needin' all these years, nice li'l ol' piece o' country poon to set you straight, hey?"

"I don't think so," I said.

"Oh, well, now, don't be so sure. How do you know?"

"I just know. I know what I like."

"An' what is that?"

We were back up behind the cabin again. Jim Otis sat down on the ground, plucked a grass stem to chew on, and waited for an answer.

I sat down beside him.

"Well, I want a girl to look nice, for one thing. You know, feminine. Feminine and sharp-looking. I guess . . . well, she should be clean, and her hair looking soft and nice and natural, and not too much makeup, you know—just enough to look natural."

"Natural," repeated Jim Otis.

"Yeah, but . . . in a sharp sort of way. With-it, you know. She should be with-it, she should be sharp."

Carolee came out of the cabin with a pitcher to get water for the kitchen, and I stopped talking until she had retreated back inside.

"Yeah, and she should be interesting—she should know what's going on."

"You mean what's the President doin' an' all that?"

"Well . . . what's going on. I like to be able to talk to a girl who's really sharp, you know, be able to talk to her about movies and stuff—I like to have something in common with her. There's a real excitement about coming on to a real sharp chick, you know, you really feel like you've done something if you score with her."

"Now, me, I like a woman as'll shut up when I come home from a hard day's work, myself," Jim Otis said.

"Well, you've certainly got one like that with Carolee," I said.

"Oh, Carolee," he said, dismissing her with his inflection.

"Was Leona as quiet as her?"

"Leona . . ." his eyes clouded over with concentration, and he seemed to let down his guard for an instant. "Leona was a feisty li'l ol' gal, that's for sure." He chuckled at some memory or other.

"What made you decide to marry her?"

"Mush is ready," called out Carolee from the doorway.

There was still a lot of work to do, getting the cabin ready for the two-week stay that Jim Otis was planning. Next, there was firewood to be split for the stove. Jim Otis took me around to a small padlocked utility shed behind the cabin.

"Animals," he said apologetically, nodding at the padlock as he found the key on his key ring. "Don't want some big ol' bear bustin' into my shed an' stealin' my tools when I'm down the mountain, hey?"

Leaning in the doorway of the shed, he picked up an axe and passed it out behind his back to me.

As I took it from him and felt the weight of it in my hand, and looked down the solid oak shaft at the heavy iron head, I felt a spasm of fear and exultation seize my body.

I realized I was sighting down the axe handle, directly at the base of Jim Otis' skull.

And in the instant after that tremor passed over me and my body unfroze, Jim Otis straightened up and turned around to face me. He held an axe in his hand, too, and it was identical to the one that he had given me.

"You . . . you keep two axes up here?" I said.

"I keep two of everything," he said. "Hell of a note, you get up here all alone, fixin' to stay a spell an' somethin' you need breaks down on you. I got business to do when I come up here; can't afford to spend all my time mendin' stuff."

There was no hint of an awareness of the electric current that had passed through me with such a surge that I was sure he must have felt it, too. Could he really be so careless?

I chewed myself out for missing the opportunity. I could have laid him out right then and there, made him my prisoner, taken him back.

Maybe killed him. I'd never hit anyone with the flat of an axe. I wouldn't know exactly how hard to swing.

I could still take him. The odds were equal between

us now. I had an axe, he had an axe. If he really didn't suspect anything, I'd have the element of surprise on my side. I could get in the first blow—and one blow would likely be all I'd need, if I struck so fast he didn't have a chance to parry.

We were at the woodpile. Jim Otis shanked a thick section of tree trunk down from the top of the pile and let it drop at my feet.

"Awrighty, now, Cousin Ry," he said. "Let's see if'n the city made you forget how to handle an axe, hey?"

I rolled the log up onto its butt and struck downward with all the force I could muster behind the axe blade, seeking the fault in the grain that would lay it open for me. The first few blows I struck were across the grain, and the axe chipped harmless away at the surface, stinging my hands. But on the fourth stroke I found the mark, and I could hear and feel the wood tearing away from itself as the blade ripped through it.

Jim Otis watched me intently through the entire process. I could feel his eyes gauging me, measuring the force and timing and accuracy of my downstroke, observing the strength of my grip and the angle at which I held the axe.

I found myself wondering if he had ever killed a man with an axe, and then checked my conjecture and reminded myself that as far as anyone knew, he had only one set of killings to his credit.

It was only after I had finished pounding through my first log and reached for a second, that he started to work, himself.

It seemed a casual matter, the way he rolled his log down and upended it; but I didn't think that it was. Was he just within, or just outside, my striking range, if I were to decide to make a lunge at him? I didn't know. I knew that *he* knew.

I was under observation from another quarter now, too: Carolee. She had come out of the cabin to hang up a load of wash—my yesterday's clothes from the accident—and now she stood for a moment, her shoulder and hand pressed up against the cabin wall, watching us split firewood.

It was me she was watching. And now it was my turn to stare straight ahead at what I was doing, and not look around. I was acutely aware of her scrutiny, and I couldn't meet it, nor did I understand what it was all about, any more than I understood what Jim Otis was up to with me.

I felt as if I were under glass. And I wondered again if she was a captive here, too, like me, or a captor. Was I a captive, for that matter? I still wasn't even sure of that.

I knew I wasn't going to get a straight answer from Jim Otis, but if this girl wanted me to rescue her, why didn't she say so? The minds and fears of young girls are unfathomable, I decided. And my first problem was looking out for myself.

She watched for a few minutes, and then she was gone, back into the house without my realizing exactly when she left. Her eyes seemed to stay on after her, and I felt watched for a long time.

She didn't look at me at all when we came in to

stack the wood by the kitchen stove. She was preparing shuckie beans, and the pile of dried legumes on the counter beside her seemed to be all that she needed to occupy her consciousness.

Carolee dressed for dinner. She wore a knee-length dress that had buttons all the way up the front. It was navy blue, with a large floral print on it, and it had a full skirt. I couldn't imagine what had possessed her to stuff it into the backpack when we were racing to get out of Waynesville.

Her hair was tied up in a twist on the top of her head, in a way that high school girls used to think was the most grown-up and sophisticated style they could imagine, and that they used to be allowed to try out once a year for the prom. I didn't have the heart to laugh, though I felt like it.

The beans tasted like leather breeches, as my mother used to describe them. I hadn't had shuckie beans in five years—they don't make them anyplace else except in the mountains. And no one else would want to eat them, but they were one of those tastes that once you develop them you never lose. Jim Otis watched me eating with approval.

"Hey, lookee that, Carolee! There's still some traces o' the ol' country boy in Cousin Ry, scratch him deep enough," he whooped. "Yessiree, you can take the boy out o' the mountains, but you can't take the mountains out o' the boy."

Carolee smiled.

It was quite a smile. It caught me off guard. I started to say something, and it was at that moment that I realized I was just about as tongue-tied as she was.

"Mmmm-ummm, good," I finally mumbled, and bent back over my plate to shovel in another mouthful of beans.

CHAPTER 7

We got up before dawn the next morning. We were going out after a deer, but I didn't know with what. I still hadn't actually laid eyes on a gun since this whole adventure had gotten started, in spite of my suspicions. And anyway, even if Jim Otis was packing a pistol, we couldn't go out deer hunting with one handgun.

Jim Otis was up first, and in a particularly exuberant mood, even for him. He was whistling as he went out, shirtless, into the chilly autumn predawn to get wood for the stove. I looked out through the window, and I could see the whiteness of his upper body moving around the woodpile, and the little puffs of cloud from his breath, lighter than the darkness that was still good for another half hour before the sun's first rays pierced it.

With my heart beating faster than I wanted it to, I hurried over to Jim Otis' pallet, picked up his hunting jacket, and unrolled it, pressing the length of it between my chest and forearm. There was nothing in any of the pockets. No gun.

I felt foolish and frustrated, and I stood holding the

checkered jacket for a moment longer than necessary. Then I heard the rattle of a doorlatch. I started, but it was only Carolee, coming out of the bedroom. I still felt guilty and trapped—I had no reason to suppose that Carolee was any more on my side than Jim Otis was, and I wasn't about to trust her to keep a secret for me from Jim Otis.

So I didn't dare to just roll the coat back up and put it back where I'd found it. Instead, I went through an elaborate ritual of hanging the garment up on the back of a chair, then folding up Jim Otis' blanket and putting it back in the chest, and finally doing the same with my blanket. Carolee went out the front door without giving me a second look.

Just as I had gotten everything put away neatly, Jim Otis came in bearing a load of split logs. He dumped them next to the stove, glanced around the sleeping area of the room, and shot me a sharp, knowing glance. He didn't say anything; he didn't need to.

He took the coffeepot off the stove and poured us a cup, then left it sitting on the table as he lifted the stove top to put on another log. He seemed completely involved in his household chores, and barely looked up as he asked me casually:

"You'll be wantin' a gun, won't you, Cousin Ry?"

He paused just long enough to make me wonder what he was really driving at, then tossed me a broad, ingenuous grin over his shoulder, and continued: "Just in case them deer out there have 'em this year, we mought's well be prepared, hey?"

He took a sip of his coffee, made a face, set the cup down, and walked to the center of the room, right in front of the stove. He kicked aside the worn, dirty hooked rug, and pulled at a floorboard.

A section of flooring about three feet square came up in his hand—a trap door.

"Can't hunt without guns, and that's a fact," he said, reaching under the floorboards and coming out with a Winchester .30-.30 repeating rifle, which he tossed over to me.

I caught it, and immediately checked to see if it was loaded. It wasn't. When I looked back at Jim Otis, he was standing up, holding a Winchester of his own. It was pointed right at my heart, and his finger was on the trigger.

"Hey, bang bang, you're dead, Cousin Ry," he sang out, clicking the trigger of the empty gun and laughing delightedly. "Hey, wanna play cowboys an' Indians? How about cops an' robbers?"

"Got any bullets?" I asked.

"Bullets? Sure thing. Coming right up," he said. He picked up a box from the hole, then closed the trapdoor, straightened the rug, and came back over to the table.

He set the box down between us, opened it, and let me reach in for the first bullet. After I started loading, he started loading.

I no longer even had to look up and see Jim Otis laughing at me, to feel that he had an appraising eye on me all the time, taking the measure of all my skills and my reflexes.

The sun was halfway over the mountain when we started the hunt. As we passed along the top of the ridge that led up to the high wooded area, we came to a clearing that stretched away below us, back down to the stream. And at the same moment, Carolee came into sight from behind a clump of bushes, and stood for a moment at the edge of the stream, looking down into the water.

Jim Otis walked straight on, not even pausing to look down, but I paused. Carolee was naked. The new day's sun had climbed just far enough over the ridge to make the water glint with sparkling highlights, although most of the clearing between the ridge and the water was still shadow. The sun caught Carolee as she stood by the stream, and made the whiteness of her back gleam and twinkle like the highlights on the water.

My heart jumped for an instant, and then she dived into the water, splashing the sunlight, breaking the glints into thousands of shimmering dots. I walked on, quickening my step just enough to catch up to Jim Otis, and we continued along the ridge.

It was a beautiful morning! The sky was growing blue now, as the sun started to ascend higher over the hills, and a breeze kept the incredible freshness of the mountain air moving through the leaves and into our faces. We hiked for a couple of hours more, along narrow game trails, through tangled brush and open areas. I sighted down my gun at a few jays, some squirrels, and a hawk that soared high in the sky up around the top of the mountain, all the time thinking of that big buck we were going to bring down. I hoped that I'd be the one to get the first shot at it.

But whether I did or not, whether we even brought

down a deer or not, it just felt so good to be out there. If we didn't get one today, we'd get one tomorrow. Jim Otis was a good hunter—one of the best. And, hell, I knew how to handle myself in the woods, too. I hadn't forgotten it all—you never do, I decided. It was locked in deep; it was a basic part of a mountaineer's unconscious, like eating shuckie beans.

For the first time since I'd moved to the city, I could really understand what people meant when they talked about how great it was to get out into the country. Oh, I'd gone hunting on a few weekends with guys I knew from the city, gone to somebody or other's lodge for the weekend, or driven out for the day and parked the car on the side of the road; but I was always bored; couldn't wait to get back to the city again.

We took up positions about twenty feet apart on the side of a hill with good tree cover, overlooking a decent-sized clearing in the valley below, and waited. From time to time I would shoot an inquiring glance over to Jim Otis on my right; and each time my eyes even flickered toward him, he was aware of it, as he was of every other motion in the woods around him. He would nod back, or give me an encouraging thumbs-up gesture.

The deer came through the clearing about two hours later, a fine eight-point buck. I put my gun up to my shoulder and sighted at the animal, then hesitated for an instant and looked over at Jim Otis.

His gun was cradled in his arms, still—ready to bring it up to his cheek in a split second, if he had to, but waiting to give me a chance at the first shot. He looked sharply at me, his brow creasing with impatience.

The buck suddenly sensed that something was wrong. His body was already tensed for flight as the safety on my gun clicked, and he was fleeing before I could squeeze the trigger.

I followed him through my gunsight to the edge of the clearing. I sensed rather than saw Jim Otis raising his gun, but I squeezed off my shot first, and just in time, catching the buck at the far end of the clearing. He ran about two more strides into the woods, out of our sight, then crashed with a heavy thud. The bullet hole was right behind his ear, we found, when we came up to him.

If I had hoped Jim Otis would tell me it was a nice shot, I was disappointed; but he nodded his head with what I took to be appreciation, so I counted that as being almost as good.

Jim Otis opened his hunting coat, and I noticed to my surprise, that he had *two* hunting knives in two sheaths on his belt. On reflection, I didn't know why I should be surprised—it was the same thing again, two of everything. Every weapon, anyway. One for him and one for me. He unsnapped the loops on both sheaths, and tossed me one knife.

I caught it by the handle, and tested the blade on my thumb. It was very sharp. I was gradually acquiring an arsenal of weapons, it seemed—an arsenal matched exactly by Jim Otis.

He gestured with his knife at the dead buck, and I turned my attention back to it. It was a fine big animal, a worthy kill— a beautiful sight.

"Your kill, Cousin," said Jim Otis.

He squatted on his haunches beside me, cleaning his nails with his hunting knife, while I slit the deer and gutted it. As I felt his ever-appraising eyes on me, I was sure that I was not doing it as expertly as he would have. But I got it done. I looked at him for a sign of approval or disapproval, but I got neither. Just the observation, just the scrutiny. Always that keen observation: he was taking everything in. What his judgment was, I don't know, and he never gave any indication.

He took the deer's liver, wrapped it in a piece of oilcloth, and put it in his pocket. Then we cut a pole, lashed the hooves of the carcass to it, and started home.

Whatever Jim Otis may have thought, I was well enough pleased with myself. I'd shown that I could still take care of myself in the woods. I'd made the kill with a clean shot, and was on my way home with the trophy. Even carrying a fullgrown deer, my steps felt buoyant, and the walk back no more than an exuberant stretch of the legs.

I observed less on the way home than I had on the way out, but the woods felt just as full of wonder and excitement. My mind was taken up with reliving the day's events. I thought of nothing else but the big buck gliding through the clearing, pausing to sniff at the air; the sudden fear and effortless propulsion into motion; the shot . . . I heard the sound of his body crashing down in the woods over and over again in my mind; I saw myself looking down at the carcass at my feet; I heard Jim Otis saying *Your kill, Cousin.* My imagination floated back away from my body; I was watching myself tramping through the mountains with Jim Otis, the two of us together, carrying the gutted stag between us. I was enveloped in a warm glow of comradeship and self-satisfaction.

As we neared home, I suddenly passed into another sensation, one that I couldn't identify at first. A tingling, a faint sense of apprehension, not danger, just the feeling of another presence. What could it be? I looked around, but there was no one else in sight.

At last I realized that we were walking past the spot where I had seen Carolee preparing to bathe that morning. I looked down at the flat rock between the two clumps of bushes, and a vision of Carolee's glowing rounded ass suddenly came into sharp, almost blinding focus in my brain. I looked back over my shoulder at the deer's head, hanging limply and upside down, and spoke to myself sharply. After all, I hadn't been in the mountains for *that* long.

But all the rhythm of my feeling was broken, and I walked the rest of the way back to the cabin in a state of nervous, irritated anticipation.

We hung the deer from a tree behind the cabin. Carolee came out to watch, and I felt acutely self-conscious. I could tell that all my movements were just a little forced, just a little stagy. I was swaggering too much, but I didn't quite know how to stop: I seemed to have forgotten how to act naturally. And when Carolee turned around and went back inside the cabin, I felt deflated.

We washed up, and she had dinner ready for us.

Lentil soup and biscuits, from the stock of dried provisions in the cabin pantry.

"Tomorrow . . . venison, hey, Cousin Ry?" Jim Otis exulted with his mouth full of sourdough biscuit, slurring his words a little as a few dry crumbs tumbled down his chin.

"Damn right," I said, thumping the table, a little sheepish but proud. "We're gonna have us some real meat on the table!"

"You can bet your last red nickel we are, Cousin. Real red meat an' some real good ol' times, hey? This calls for a celebration!"

He reached under the table and brought up an earthenware jug.

"Hey, how 'bout it, Cousin? From my private stock," he said. "Brought in special for tonight's big celebration, the finest aged, bonded, blended, *im*-ported, *ex*-ported, home comfort, high quality and ree-nowned Panther Piss."

I couldn't believe my own rush of excitement. A jug of Jim Otis Churchwarden's moonshine. I'd seen them often, back when I was a kid—at least a few times, and heard about them all my life—but I'd never been offered a drink from one before. None of us kids ever were. That was one of the unwritten rules for separating the men from the boys, one of the final rites of passage for mountain manhood. It came after coon hunting with the hounds at night, after getting drunk on 3.2 beer behind the store during the Saturday night square dances, and asking a girl your own age to dance with you in a moonlight dance instead of being dragged into it by an old lady—they were the square dances where the last part of the call was, "then you kiss her in the moonlight if you dare."

It came right after being taken into Waynesville for a first piece of poon. It came just before you went into the Army; and playing euchre with the men in the back of the store came after you got out, or on your first furlough. But I wasn't properly one of the boys—I was the storekeeper's son, and I went to college instead of into the Army, so I missed out on the poontang in Waynesville, and the white lightning. And I had never come back home to lay claim to any of the symbols of my coming of age in Passaqua County.

And I had never wanted to. They were all rituals that were at the heart of a way of life I had desired passionately to forget. Hunting was one thing—going out into the woods and bringing down a deer for your table. But the rest—the crudeness, the backwardness, the incredible perversion of values that could justify marrying a thirteen-year-old girl—and then killing her.

And I don't mean to say that I didn't have a kind of sentimental spot in my heart for old Jim Otis—sure I did, I would admit that freely enough. I was as human as the next guy. But it wasn't enough to make me forget all the rest.

Nevertheless, I found myself actually trembling with excitement and anticipation when Jim Otis uncorked the jug and poured a generous portion of white lightning into a tin cup for me.

Then he poured an identical shot for himself.

"Well, here's to that fine ol' deer that Cousin Ry shot hisself," he said, holding his cup aloft.

I realized that I had been waiting for him to say

something like that, wanting Carolee to know that it had been me who had brought the deer down, but not wanting to say so myself. I looked at her out of the corner of my eye, but could detect no visible reaction.

"To the deer," I said.

Jim Otis threw off his shot at one gulp, and I tried to do the same. It was a disaster.

The liquor had gotten only halfway down my throat when the explosion hit.

It seemed to go off every way at once. Burning down into my stomach, bubbling back up as I coughed, gasped, and choked, dribbling out of the corners of my mouth, gushing out of my nose, making my eyes glaze over. It rocketed through my chest, causing my ribs to twang like bowstrings. It made my fingers tingle and my ears buzz. It took the place of blood in my heart and air in my lungs.

I think I swallowed most of it. But perhaps it just seemed that way. Perhaps I couldn't believe that my head would be reeling so after just one drink, unless I had definitely gotten most of it down.

When I could breathe again, I looked up at Jim Otis. I expected him to be laughing at me, and he was. I did not look at Carolee.

"Still alive, Cousin?" he asked. "Got a mite bit of kick to 'er, ain't she? Here, have some more."

He refilled my cup and his.

I plunged right back at it gamely, but more prudently. I took only a small swallow.

Even that was plenty. I got it down without too much spluttering, but I could feel my face starting to tingle, and I could tell from the warmth that it must be turning a bright pink.

I felt warm all over. Rubbery and limp, but warm.

"Hey, Carolee, honey, you want to get my banjo?" Jim Otis said.

She went over to get it from the corner. As she bent over the banjo case in the soft light and deep shadows of the kerosene lamp, in her snug-fitting jeans and loose flannel shirt, all I could see before my eyes was that bright, heartstopping flash of nakedness I had seen by the stream in the first light of morning. But when she turned and walked back carrying the instrument, the vision vanished.

I couldn't even imagine her naked from the front. What did a fifteen-year-old girl look like? She had some sort of breasts, I could tell that even with her clothes on; but with the loose-fitting shirt and a bra, who could tell what the shape of them was, or how big they were? Did she have pubic hair yet? When did girls get it? When had I gotten it?

It was too hard to remember, and I wasn't in a mood for pushing my brain, not with a third cup of moonshine in my hands. It was hard to think about pubic hair at all, for that matter, when you looked at those chubby cheeks and round, girlish face. I took another sip of moonshine as Jim Otis tuned up his banjo and started playing his weird haunting mountain chords.

CHAPTER 8

It was a beautiful morning. There was a bright shaft of sunlight through the window over my head, and dust particles were floating in it. There was clean mountain air and a fresh-killed deer hanging from a tree outside and the smell of coffee on the stove.

And I had a hangover.

My head pounded and I felt dizzy and queasy the first time I tried to stand up. I sank to my knees and let my head flop down on my chest. After resting in that position for a few moments, I started over, much more slowly. This time I made it to the table and sat down heavily, propping myself up with both elbows. Carolee put a steaming hot cup of coffee in front of me, and gave me a sympathetic half-smile. I looked at the coffee for a long time before I made the decision to attempt shifting my balance enough to try and pick it up.

Yet, for all that, I couldn't really say I felt bad. I actually retained a lot of the sense of well-being that I'd drunk myself into the night before. And a lot of the good feeling for Jim Otis—my cousin Jim Otis.

Now we'd chopped wood together, hunted together, shared weapons together, eaten and gotten drunk together. He had offered me his moonshine—surely a token of trust and comradeship. Even the hangover was a kind of a badge of honor.

The coffee started to bring me around, gradually. Jim Otis joined me at the table as I started my second cup.

"Hey, champ, how ya feelin'?" he asked.

"Mmm . . . rummm . . ." I muttered, nodding my head very, very slowly.

"Got a bit of kick to 'er, ain't she?"

"Kick? Ooh . . . I feel like I've been shot out of a cannon."

"Yeh, she'll do that, she will. But she sure irons the kinks out."

"If she doesn't iron the rest of you out at the same time."

"Hey, you're gonna be all right. You just have one more li'l ol' cup o' that black coffee, and then go down an' soak your head in the crick for a spell; that'll perk you right up. Ol' mountain water give you that head, ol' mountain water should oughta clear it up. We got us a lot to do today, Cousin."

"I feel a little better," I said, draining the cup.

"Sure you do," said Jim Otis.

I went down to the stream and bathed in the icy running water, and brought myself to the point where I was ready to start the day's work, if I didn't have to move too fast.

Dressing the deer, fortunately, was a nice steady job that didn't involve too much moving from place to place; and after a morning of that, I was feeling more or less my old self again.

"Come on," Jim Otis said after lunch.

"Where to?" I asked, but he just led the way, back of the cabin, in a northerly direction and up an extremely steep path that I hadn't seen before, to the top of a knoll, through a narrow crevice about ten feet long, between two large rocks and finally to a flat, rocky area, at the foot of a small waterfall and on the bank of a shallow but clear and fast-flowing mountain stream.

In the middle of it was a brick firebox, with the holding tank of a gas hot-water heater embedded in its surface. Copper pipes came out of the top of the hot-water heater, and led to a complicated series of containers, pipes, and pieces of tubing. I didn't understand it all, but I got the total picture well enough to grasp what it was. At the foot of the last pipe was an earthenware jug.

"Well, what d'ye think, Cousin?" he asked, waving his hand at the array.

I was astounded. And overwhelmed. And bewildered.

"Look . . . I . . . look here, Jim Otis . . . Cousin . . . er . . ." I stammered. "This is . . . well, it's incredible. But it's . . . aren't you forgetting . . . I'm still . . . that is . . . well, you know. Hell, I'm still a federal cop. I mean . . . this puts me in kind of a difficult situation. We've been getting along fine, so far, and you're my cousin and all, and I don't want to double-cross you after you've taken me into your confidence like this, but . . ."

Jim Otis threw back his head and laughed.

"Why sure, Cousin," he said. "I ain't fixin' to cause you no embarrassment, now, not ol' Cousin Jim Otis. I tell you what, Cousin, you just relax a little bit an' forget about bein' a big ol' cop for a couple o' weeks, a few days, just while we're both here, an' when the time comes to remember it we'll both think about it then, hey? Way I figger it, where you boys is plannin' on sendin' me, I ain't gonna have no more use for this ol' rig, nohow, leastways not for a long, long time."

He paused and looked long and hard at his creation. Then he opened the firebox door and pushed in a couple of large logs.

"Came up early this mornin' an' fired 'er up," he said. "While you was still sleepin' it off." The heat from the firebox was tremendous already. Jim Otis shifted the position of the logs with a poker, checked a pressure gauge on top of the hot-water heater, and started talking again, half to himself.

"Yup, I know they ain't much point in doin' none o' this, either—makin' good whiskey as'll never be sold, never be drunk, never be run across no state line in no supercharged Roadrunner with a concealed tank in the trunk. Funny, though, don't seem right bein' up in these hills here, 'thout mixin' up a little shine. Like passin' a little wayside chapel, an' not stoppin' to offer up a quick 'un to the Almighty."

He turned and gave me a dazzling smile at the incongruity of the comparison. "Mought's well do it together, since we're up here'th just the two of us, hey?"

he said. "Never know when an extry trade'll come in handy, 'specially when you've got all the equipment."

. "Now, just a minute, Jim Otis!" I blazed. "We've been having a hell of a good time together, I don't deny that. I'd be the first to admit it, but if you think that means I'm going to get soft and forget about my responsibilities, well, you can forget about it right now—however much friendship I may feel for you as a person. But even more than that—if you think, for one minute—if you think I'd double-cross you—turn you in and then turn around and start using this still for my own personal advantage . . ."

"Hey, now, Cousin, don't get in a pet," said Jim Otis, and his eyes were twinkling again. "I didn't mean nothin'. Man in my business, he lives with a lot 'o breakage. Takes 'er as she comes. I ain't gonna spend the next ten years o' my life in no cell grievin' about havin' no still to come back to."

He checked the temperature gauge again, and began to roll out a large glass jug, filled with a clear liquid. He gave me another conspiratorial grin over his shoulder.

"Oh, ain't gonna reform, don't you worry none about that," he said. "But they's always stills to build, even after I get out, an' they's always new places in the hills to set 'em up in."

His grin was infectious and reassuring. I couldn't stay offended, any more than I could keep on being defensive and suspicious. "I guess I would worry some if I thought you *were* going to reform," I said. "You've always been my favorite moonshiner for as far back as I can remember."

"Favorite cousin, too, you young whippersnapper," he snorted. "You sure grew up to be some kind o' handful, chasin' ol' Jim Otis into the mountains to take his ass back to jail for a li'l ol' thing like shootin' his wife. Yep, we're all right proud o' you at home, an' no mistake."

"I'm going to start law school, nights," I said. "If you stay in jail long enough, when I get my degree I'll take your case and get you out."

"Well, now, if that don't beat all. Hey, how d'ye like my still?"

"How long have you had it?" I asked.

"This'un? Oh, gettin' on 'bout three an' a half years now. I've had real good luck with this'un; ain't nobody bothered it."

"How'd you get it up here?" I asked.

"Well, for a start the trick is to come around the other side o' the mountain. I brought you up the scenic route."

I shuddered a little at the memory. "Some scenic route."

"One o' my favorites," he said.

"Yeah, I guessed there must have been an easier way," I said.

"Jeep'll take you purty near up to the top o' the ridge yonder," he said, pointing, although I wasn't really clear in which direction he was pointing—it was more a vague sweep of his arm. "Then along the ridge an' down to here with a mule—the cabin was here already, long time. All I had to bring in was tools an' supplies."

"Did you bring the mules all the way up behind the

jeep?" I asked. "I'd think that would attract quite a bit of attention, not to mention making it easy to follow you because you'd drive so slow."

"Oh, there's people up here in these hills," said Jim Otis, a strange faraway quality coming into his voice for just a moment. "People as lives here all the time, maybe don't come down off'n the mountain for three, four months at a time. They's people . . . they's people as never come down. And them as do, it's just to bring their mules into town, load 'em up with what provisions they need from outside, an' pack back up to the hills."

"And you know them? You can rent their mules?"

"Yeh, some," said Jim Otis. His mind really seemed to be elsewhere; he had to jog himself to register my question and answer it. "Yeh, they let me use 'em."

For a few seconds longer he stood, half turned away from me, still subdued and pensive. I wondered if he often wished he were one of those people. He'd certainly be in a lot less trouble, now, if he were.

"Took me a long time to put this still together," he said fondly, breaking the silence. "A long time figgerin' it out—why, there's features on this still as nobody ever thought of before, as nobody never done before. All that talk they do in them cities 'bout eecology an' conservin' energy—well, this here still damn near runs on its own energy."

He was beginning to grow more animated as he talked, and before long he was fairly prancing around, as he pointed to the various facets of its construction.

I had been looking at the apparatus, and sorting out

the various components in my mind so that I could follow them with my eyes, although I still had no idea what was what, or what made this still so special.

There was the firebox, with the hot-water heater embedded in it, that I've described before. A copper pipe came out of the top of it, and ran horizontally across to a small wooden barrel, then turned on an elbow down into the top of the barrel. Another pipe led out of the barrel top and ran, horizontally, at right angles to the first one, into a horizontal cylinder wrapped in some sort of insulation, and set up on a scaffold about six and a half feet off the ground. There was a higher platform on the scaffold, where one of the large glass jugs rested on its side above the cylinder, connected to it by a length of hose pipe.

Another copper pipe came out of the bottom of the horizontal cylinder, progressed on a slightly downhill diagonal, and into the side, near the bottom, of a large copper box. The four objects—hot water tank, barrel, horizontal cylinder, and copper box—formed the four corners of the square.

There were two more cylinders, both vertical, one on each side of the square. One was a small low copper cylinder, connected to the horizontal cylinder by another length of horizontal pipe, that came up out of the top of the one and went down into the top of the other.

Each of these vertical cylinders had a length of two-inch plastic tubing connected to it near the bottom, the other end of which was in the stream.

From the base of each cylinder, there protruded a

short copper pipe. And under each of those was an earthenware jug.

The whole apparatus was camouflaged from the air by a bower of tree limbs and boughs.

"You see them two jugs?" Jim Otis asked. "That's what's so special about this here still o' mine—it's two stills in one, an' the energy as gets throwed off by the first still runs the second.

"Now your basic still . . . ain't nothin' but heat, a boiler, an' a condenser." He pointed to the firebox, the hot-water heater, and the small copper cylinder. "That's all you need. First you take your mash—that's just corn meal an' barley malt for the fermentation; gotta have fermentation or they ain't no alcohol. You put your sour mash in the boiler, heat 'er up, an' the steam goes through your copper pipe, over to here." He tapped the condenser.

"Inside here you got your worm—that's a copper coil, some copper tubing, just keeps windin' an' windin' around in a spiral from top to bottom. Steam comes down into it, an' your cold water comin' into the condenser—worm tub, some calls it—cools the outer surface o' the worm, steam changes back into liquid, an' that's your shine."

He went over the basics fairly quickly, obviously eager to get on to describing his innovations, but patiently enough so that I could grasp them. I nodded my head as he pointed to the apparatus related to each step.

"I made them copper containers myself," he said. "Tinned the inner surfaces with solder. Took me a couple o' months to get 'em right.

"Alcohol boils faster'n water, so's your vapor is gonna have more alcohol in it when it cools down to a liquid again. Hotter the fire, more water boils, lower proof your liquid is gonna be. Fella been doin' this for a while, he can tell what kind o' proof he's gettin' just by how hot the fire is."

"How hot do you let it get?" I asked. "You don't seem to have any thermometer or any kind of gauge to measure the proof."

"Shit, no. I can tell by feel an' by taste, that's all an ol' country boy needs. Tell by bangin' on the pipes, too." He picked up an iron rod and tapped the pipe that led out of the boiler. "Sounds holler, rings like a banjo or an ol' coon hound's bay, you got a real nice high percentage of alky-hol goin' through there. Do it sound kinda dull an' flat, like a momma's tit, you got yourself a lot o' water in that vapor. Anyway, first time through, it's gonna be purty thin stuff.

"One thing you can do about that is to use a doubler—" He gestured at the barrel. "That's a doubler there. Most stills have 'em. See, your barrel's half full o' water." He tapped it, and it made a heavy thud. "Vapor comes into it, heats the water. Purty soon ol' water's heated right up to the boilin' point of alcohol. Water stays, alcohol goes on bein' vapor an' heads right on through to the condenser.

"Ho-kay, then." Jim Otis was really animated now, building up more and more excitement over what he was about to tell me; and there was something more, too. There was a warmth in his voice, almost a tenderness; it made me feel close to him, and at the same time it disconcerted me. I concentrated on the still.

"Now, even with the doubler, you still get a product as has to be distilled one more time, bring it up to a hundred proof or more. Everyone does. What your reg-'lar moonshiner, or reg'lar commercial distiller for that matter, does now is to fire up the firebox again, pour the stuff back in, an' start over. Twice as much time, twice as much work, twice as much fuel, just for one batch o' whiskey.

"That's where this comes in." He tapped the horizontal cylinder. "I got another hot-water heater in here, with a copper coil inside it."

He pointed to the copper tubing that came out of the doubler and into the horizontal cylinder. "Vapor goes in here, goes through this coil, it gets pretty hot. Then I fill the tank itself with moonshine that's been distilled once, so's it already got a purty high alcohol content. Now, then, you got all this here alky-hol swimmin' 'round in a tank as has got this hot coil in, an' the insulation 'round the tank holdin' the heat in— the boilin' point o' alcohol bein' so much lower than water—a hundred an' seventy-three degrees, for pure stuff—your waste heat from the distillin' process o' the first still is enough to drive this second still. It boils the alcohol, an' the steam runs off into a second condenser."

He indicated the vertical boiler with the jug under it.

"And there's a coil inside that, too, like the other condenser?"

"Exactly."

I concentrated hard, trying to get it all straight in my

mind. "The second still, then . . . it operates on something like the same principle as the doubler."

He beamed at me. "That ain't bad. Yeah, it works on the same principle o' alcohol boilin' lower than water. So even with the heat loss from the steam travelin' through the pipe, it's got enough when she gets to the second still to boil what it's gotta boil." He caressed the insulation on the side of the second still lovingly. I touched it gingerly. It was cool. All the heat was really being thrown back into the still. I put my hand near the copper pipe where it entered, and then where it exited from the second still, and I didn't have to touch it to feel the heat waves emanating from it.

"And the vapor from the first distilling goes through that coil, and on into the first condenser."

"Kee-rect."

"Then what's this other thing—the square copper box between the second still and the first condenser?"

"I made that box, too. That's my preheater. There's another coil as runs through the bottom o' that box. You puts your sour mash in the box, an the heat that's left in the vapor—it's already startin' to liquefy—as it goes through the coil, starts heatin' the mash. Time you've finished with one boilerful, you got yourself another half on its way to boilin', an' you just pour it into the boiler. Saves more time, more fuel. That's why I can make as much whiskey with one still as most moonshiners can with three—gives me a real big-time, big-volume operation in a space small enough so's I can camouflage it easy."

We spent the rest of the day making moonshine. I helped out some, feeding the fire, using a pulley to lift the bottles of low-proof, once-distilled liquor into position on the scaffold to feed the second still. But Jim Otis did most of the work himself. The still was his pride and joy, and it clearly made him uncomfortable to see other hands on it. As I watched it in operation, and began to understand how it worked a little more fully, I marveled at the simplicity and ingenuity of Jim Otis' innovations. They seemed so simple, once you understood the principle—harnessing of the waste energy that was a natural by-product of the operation—but what a lot of thought must have gone into coming up with them! How much close observation, how much contemplation of the properties of a still . . . it had to be a labor of love.

There were magnificent venison steaks for supper that night, followed by a couple of mugs of moonshine whiskey. I was becoming much more adept at getting it down without gulping and sputtering. I still shuddered every time the impact hit me—it was as if I had a funny bone in my throat, and the whiskey kicked it a good one every time it went past. But I didn't feel like a rank beginner, and I didn't have to feel embarrassed in front of Carolee.

Another thing that didn't happen was that I didn't descend into an immediate drunken stupor this time. I felt mellow but lively; I felt like kicking up my heels.

I was hoping Jim Otis would play the banjo again, so I could sing along. But instead he got to his feet abruptly, and didn't call for the banjo.

"I guess I'll go out an' check on the still," he said.

I was left sitting at the table with Carolee. I felt

like I ought to say something to her. It might have been a good opportunity to get some more information about Jim Otis out of her, but I didn't feel like prying. It seemed too much like work, and anyway, I just felt too good to ruin the evening with a lot of snooping. I sat and cast sidelong glances, trying to think of something to talk about.

Finally I gave up on being original.

"Well, hi," I said.

"Hi," she said.

"You don't talk very much, do you?" I said.

She agreed by not saying anything. An uncertain smile flickered across her face for an instant, a look of adolescent confusion. Then her expression became impassive again—a mountain woman's expression that was neither young nor old, but timeless, unchanged on the faces of these women for generations.

I was in an expansive mood, though, and I decided to try and draw her out.

"I guess it must be hard for you to feel you can't really assert yourself, when you're cooped up in a place with people who are so much older than you," I said.

"I ain't so much younger," she said. "Folks is all pretty much the same, whatever age they are."

"Oh, sure," I said. "I didn't mean . . ."

But I trailed off. I had meant it, of course, and there was no point trying to cover it up with a lot of words. Better to just let it drop.

"Ain't my place to talk a whole lot here," she said. "I got no claim on this house."

"And Jim Otis?"

"Jim Otis was my sister's man," she said.

Her thirteen-year-old sister. I shook my head, and tossed off the rest of what was in my cup. The liquor still burned all the way down, and I felt warm all the way through.

I set the cup down and used my sleeve to wipe my mouth, rubbing it into the shape of a benign, goofy smile, that settled in on my face. I looked back over at Carolee.

I don't know what it was that I suddenly saw different; but, whatever it was, it was enough.

I know what I did. I stood up, took Carolee by both hands, and pulled her up to her feet.

She rose up to meet me, and I pulled her inside my arms and kissed her. She pressed closely against my body, and I held her motionless for as long as I could stand it. I still felt, at that moment, that as long as we stood still it could be the same as if nothing had happened.

She didn't move, either, just kept her arms around me, one right across my shoulder blades, the other about six inches farther down. Her fists were clenched.

Her temple was pressed against my cheek, a few wisps of hair tickling under my nose. I moved my head slightly; she moved hers slightly. I didn't stop; neither did she, and we kissed again, deep and open-mouthed this time.

My hands moved up and down her back, pressing one part of her body and then another tight in against me. Her fists flew open and her fingers dug into my back. I was completely absorbed in her, and in the moment: so much so that I wasn't even scheming as to when would be the precise moment to move on to the next step.

That was ironic. With all the girls I knew back in Washington, the lot of whom were at least as experienced as I was, if not more so, and sexually aggressive enough to know exactly what they wanted and what they were going to do, I was always trying to finesse them. I was always thinking about getting a little edge, turning them on a little more and then a little more, till at last they were on their backs. And with this young girl . . . it was all different. One moment flowed into the next, and I don't think I ever knew what I was doing until I was doing it. All I know for sure is that where even flirting with a fifteen-year-old girl would have seemed gross and distasteful to me right up until that moment, now every touch seemed as right and natural as anything I'd ever done in my life.

We didn't even pull apart enough to look at each other until we were in the bedroom. Then I saw her eyes, mostly. Her face was flushed and glistening with sweat, but still the same smooth round young girl's face. It hadn't changed. But in her eyes . . . I saw that look that had always been there, but that I'd kept my distance from—that timeless, ageless, eternal quality of the mountains.

I unbuttoned the first two buttons of her shirt. She did the rest, while I undressed myself. She took off her underwear when she was under the covers.

We rolled together. She hugged me tightly, and I held her, my sex rubbing against hers in an instinctive, rhythmical pattern, gradually sliding between her thighs, and then inside her.

There was a moment of resistance, and then resistance suddenly gave way with a sound that I had never heard before, but I knew well enough what it was.

I had never done it with a virgin before. For a fleeting instant I felt betrayed—*why didn't she tell me*? Then I came, and she gasped several times.

I woke up alone. No hangover, and I remembered everything from the night before perfectly. But I still had to sit up, rub my brow, and try to piece it all together.

Why was I so surprised that she was a virgin? Because of her sister? Because I assumed that she and Jim Otis . . . ? Well, I could be sure about that now, anyway. She and Jim Otis hadn't. Why choose me, then, and how was he going to take it? What was ahead for the three of us, sharing this cabin? And what was I doing with a fifteen-year-old hillbilly girl?

I began to tune into sounds from the next room. It was Carolee, bustling about the kitchen, singing to herself.

I was truly afraid to walk through that door, but I knew that I had to face it. And, at last, I did.

Jim Otis was not in sight. That made it easier, but even so, my first impulse was to grab a cup of coffee and go outside to look for him—not to confront Carolee at all. Instead, I sat down at the table.

Carolee looked up at me from the stove, and I suddenly felt more at home than I ever had in my life, anywhere. I wanted to curl up under the table like a cat, and hug myself.

She still didn't say anything, but now her silence had a different quality to it. Humming to herself was part of it, but there was a lot more. Her whole being was different. She filled the cabin now, where before she had been no more than a shadow in it. Now its contours seemed to mold themselves to her, and she assimilated her surroundings with a comfortable, proprietary air.

In a way, I felt myself at the center of it; but in a much more basic way, she was her own center. And I was part of the sphere that her new sense of herself had drawn around her.

She brought me coffee, and breakfast—hot biscuits and gravy. She dodged away when I reached out to touch her, but there was an indulgent, proprietary acceptance even in that. Everything in its time, she seemed to be saying. Everything in its time.

She sat down with me, and we ate breakfast together, quietly. The feeling was so homelike that I had almost forgotten, until it suddenly hit me like a blow from behind, that this was in fact somebody else's cabin, and he wasn't around.

"Where's Jim Otis?" I asked.

"He went off," Carolee said. "He went off this morning. Took him a rifle an' a Bowie knife an' went off into the mountains. Said you was to come an' get him if'n you wanted him. He left those for you."

She pointed over to the far corner of the room, and

I followed the direction of her finger. Propped up against the wall were the Winchester and the Bowie knife Jim Otis had given me to hunt with. On the floor in front of them was a box of bullets.

CHAPTER 9

It was hard to grasp exactly what she had said. And just as hard to make any sense of her attitude. She didn't seem to have one; she was just reporting the message.

I spoke numbly. I felt as if I were being lowered into a swamp with a weight around my neck, and my words came out with a great effort.

"What time did he go?"

"'Bout two hours ago. When I first got up. He was all set to leave then, an' he just told me to tell you, an' then he left."

"What else did he say?"

"Nothing else."

"Which way he was going?"

"No."

"Why didn't you tell me before?"

"I told you now. I wanted you to have a good breakfast first. He's got enough of a start on you, stoppin' for breakfast ain't gonna make no difference. 'Sides, I didn't even know did you wanna go chasin' after him."

"You didn't— What did you think I was going to do?"

"I guess you'd do whatever you was gonna do," she shrugged.

"Did you know about this before? Did you know what he was planning?"

She shook her head.

"Does he . . . do you think he means it?"

But I was pretty sure I knew the answer to that.

"Don't know. I guess so, yeah. I guess probably so."

"But do you think he plans to . . . he wants to . . . he plans to wait for me out there and kill me? Or is he just trying to escape?"

She thought for a minute. "If I was you I wouldn't go after him."

"Of course I'll go after him," I said, but I wasn't as sure as I sounded, or as I wanted to be. "But that's crazy."

Carolee said nothing.

"Well, it is. He'd have to be crazy to just go hide in the woods and wait for me."

"Reckon he's pretty crazy," she said.

"He gave me his word!" I said, aware of how ridiculous I sounded. "We were going to . . . he was going to go in with me and give himself up. He gave me his word!"

I knew I sounded ridiculous, but I felt betrayed just the same. I felt like crying. I had finally started to trust him. More than that, I had started to believe in the old Jim Otis again. I had found myself coming around to accepting all the old feelings I'd had when I was a kid, looking up to him for all the things he could do and his easy, devil-may-care way of doing them. I had started to feel excited, even honored, by having him recognize me and treat me as a buddy, just as I'd dreamed of it in the old days. And even more than that, I had allowed myself to feel that Jim Otis was starting to see me as a grown-up now, as almost an equal.

And all the time, all that testing, that appraising . . . he was just setting me up!

I'd show him. Did he think I was going to chicken out?

"Of course I'll go after him," I said again. "That's my job. It's what I came here for."

It wasn't, exactly. And the bravado in my words rang pretty thin in my own ears.

"How could you have any respect for me if I didn't?" I asked, fishing for a response.

"It's between you and him," Carolee said.

I was wary as I left the cabin by the front door, expecting anything. It could be that Jim Otis was waiting in ambush right there. It could be that he'd want to put a quick end to the show—just gun me down right there, in front of Carolee.

I might never get out of the cabin at all. I might open the door and be knocked back inside by a slug in my guts, my blood flowing across the cabin floor at Carolee's feet. It could happen. Just the loud crack of a rifle as I opened the door, and that would be it.

I couldn't afford to panic. But I would have to start being on my guard right away—I couldn't afford to be careless, not even at the first step.

I kicked the door open and rolled out to the right;

and as I regained my feet I ran a low, zigzagging course over to the protection of the woodpile. There was no burst of gunfire. I looked back and saw Carolee standing in the doorway, watching me, and I felt foolish as hell. I made my face a mask of grim determination, and stalked off toward the woods.

I acted out that grim-visaged display of purpose so completely that it sustained me for a good fifteen minutes into the woods. Then it suddenly collapsed, and about the same time I was struck by the realization of how unprepared for a task like this I really was. Then I started to get scared.

It came upon me very quickly. One minute I was striding along, checking the path at my feet for a sign, and the next I stood still and tense, suddenly aware that a sinking, hollow feeling had taken over my insides, and that the blood had left my fingers and toes and was now receding from my arms and legs.

And then I could no longer even stand up. I sat down by the side of the path, pulled my knees up against my chest, and trembled.

The next thing I knew, the trembling became more and more intense, and I rolled over on my stomach, then picked myself up on my hands and knees and was violently sick.

As I heaved, I wondered if Jim Otis was watching me at that moment.

What in God's name did I think I was doing, matching myself, out in the middle of the mountains, against a mountain man? I didn't know anything about reading signs or following a trail. I didn't know anything about the mountains, and I had no idea what Jim Otis' favorite trails or resting places were.

He knew all about me, though. There was no doubt in my mind about that. All that scrutiny, those eyes I had felt dissecting my skills in every move I made. Jim Otis knew everything he needed to know about my nerves, my reflexes, my skill with a gun and a knife.

I wondered, wildly, what conclusions he had drawn from his tests. Had he headed for the woods to play this deadly tracking game with me because he felt he had a worthy adversary, or was it because he figured he had an easy target?

My stomach hurt, my throat and nostrils felt raw, and my mouth had the vile taste of vomit in it. I realized that I had brought nothing with me, not even a canteen.

Briefly, I thought about going back to the cabin for some supplies, but I knew I couldn't do that. I couldn't let Carolee see me in this condition. I'd go on. I could get water from the stream—and I wasn't going to be able to eat, anyway. My stomach wouldn't allow it.

I picked a direction without thinking, and set out again. I must have been in a state of barely suppressed hysteria all that morning. My actions were completely erratic. Fear alternated with frustration, prudence with recklessness, my training and common sense with an irrational desire to rush in and have it over with. I alternated between creeping furtively from tree to tree and striding wildly and noisily along game trails, my head down and my mind a blank. I had no sense at all of exactly where I was, until suddenly I pitched into the clearing where Jim Otis and I had brought down the deer.

I stopped there on the hillside, brought up short by the familiarity of it. My heart pounded and my nerve ends bristled as I looked down into the clearing, almost as if I expected Jim Otis to sweep gracefully across it as the buck had done.

I sat down to rest and rethink my position. But I was too nervous to rest, and my brain jumped with too many memories to permit me to make plans.

I saw myself out on this same hillside with Jim Otis, just three days earlier, clutching the stock of the same rifle I clutched now, the gun that Jim Otis had given me. I saw myself waiting then with eager anticipation, but still savoring every moment of the wait, thrilled and reassured by the presence of Jim Otis Churchwarden at my side.

But who was it that I was looking at, on that hillside? It wasn't me; it was someone else. It was young fifteen-year-old Ry Justice of Clove Valley, with his first gun, out for his first hunt with the men. It was a Ry Justice who never was. Not Ry Justice the storekeeper's son, the one who was never quite fast enough or quite clever enough to be included when the real excitement started. Not fifteen-year-old Ry Justice who got beaten up in a schoolyard fight by a fourteen-year-old boy who kicked him hard in the shin at the same instance he threw his first punch, a tactic that Ry would never have thought of, and if he had thought of it, would never have dared to use. That Ry Justice had an instinct that told him that whatever he did, the other person would manage to retaliate with something worse. Would anticipate with something worse, in fact—if he so much as thought of kicking the other kid in the shins, he was sure to get kicked in the balls. Better just to absorb the punishment, because then there might not be as much.

That Ry Justice was the one who had never had the nerve to sneak out behind the bushes with a girl. Once he had kissed Mollie Travers in a moonlight dance, and for weeks afterward he had thought of her as his sweetheart. But he had never had the nerve to follow it up, and when she went out to the cemetery with Gene Hines, and all the kids started whispering about it at school, he had felt shamed and betrayed.

That Ry Justice was the one who had always stood in the back of the kids who hung around Jim Otis Churchwarden, in spite of the fact that he was some kind of cousin to him.

And he hardly even drank any of the beer he was occasionally able to steal from his father's store and use as his price of admission to the gang of boys his age whom he longed to be accepted by. And when he went away to college, he had felt it as the ultimate defeat.

That was not the young Ry I saw on the hillside. I was looking at a young Ry who had been singled out of the gang by Jim Otis as special, as the likeliest youngster, chosen ahead of six-foot two-inch Win Bottom; or Freddie Shaw, who was the first kid in the ninth grade to learn how to chew tobacco without choking; or Jack Murphy, who they said had gotten the schoolteacher drunk and felt her up. It was young

Ry Justice who had been brought up to Jim Otis' private hideaway in the mountains, had drunk moonshine with him and tended his still with him. It was young Ry Justice whom Jim Otis had given a gun to, a Winchester .30 –.30 repeating rifle just like his own.

That was the figure I saw on the hillside. Young Ry Justice chosen from all others to sit at the side of his idol, to be allowed to take the first shot, to walk home in the late afternoon sunshine with Jim Otis, carrying a deer between them.

And what did any of that have to do with Ryland Justice the college graduate with the swinging bachelor apartment in Washington, D.C.? The prelaw student majoring in sociology and criminology? The police-trained small-arms marksman and self-defense student, seventh in his class in target shooting and green belt in karate? Ryland Justice who had seduced nine women since he arrived in Washington, D.C., and that wasn't even counting below-the-waist making out at parties?

What about the Ryland Justice who had come back to Passaqua County to do a job and take a murderer into custody?

I saw the photographs of Leona Churchwarden again, remembered my fear and my suspicion, and my original decision to play along with Jim Otis until I could find an opening and turn the tables. It was all getting less and less vivid, more jumbled, and harder to keep straight.

I don't know what part of it was waking and what part was sleeping, but I do know that when I snapped out of my reverie, the late afternoon sun was starting to diffuse itself and color the sky, and I felt cold and hungry. And I know that somewhere in all that jumble of thoughts and dreams and memories, there was the vision of young Ry, in his new glory, finally finding the nerve to take a girl and go out behind the bushes.

As I retraced my steps back to the cabin, I felt what I had felt ever since I had been brought up here: that sense of being under a constant close scrutiny.

Now, however, the feeling was much more ominous, unseen, and frightening. But it was every bit as real a presence as when Jim Otis had actually been by my side, looking down over my shoulder.

I felt betrayed, but I wasn't sure exactly how. Or which one of my selves was the victim.

And I felt myself in deadly peril. That was a sensation that was very clear and unequivocal.

CHAPTER 10

It was dark when I got back to the cabin, and I approached it warily, not knowing what to expect inside, whether I might find Jim Otis there, holding Carolee captive, or what. I was prepared for anything. It even flashed through my mind that the whole thing might have been some kind of weird practical joke, and I might walk in to find Jim Otis and Carolee sitting at the dinner table as if nothing had happened.

But I didn't really expect that. An ambush was a lot more likely. I crept around to the back of the cabin and looked, as well as I could without revealing myself, through the small window,

I didn't see any sign of Jim Otis. All I could see was Carolee stopping by the stove to give a few stirs to something simmering in a large pot on top of it; and I could smell the aroma of a venison stew.

It was inviting; but I still wanted to be wary. I watched through the window for a few minutes longer, trying to detect any sign of tension or uneasiness in Carolee, any clue to a possible ambush; but I saw nothing. Hunger, and the smell of that stew, was looming larger for me than my capacity for distrust. And I couldn't find any indication that I had grounds for distrust.

I thought I had moved silently around the building, but the door opened for me as I came up to it. I leaped backward, and started to bring up my gun, but it was only Carolee. Even so, I was still trembling. I stood where I was for a moment, glaring at her suspiciously. But there was nothing in her expression except welcome, and it began to dawn on me that I was no more likely safe from ambush standing framed in the doorway of the cabin, presenting a target from outside, than I was by going inside. I went on in.

Carolee offered up her face to be kissed, but I looked around the room first to make sure the coast was clear, and when I turned back to her she had gotten angry and walked away.

"What's the matter?" I asked.

She shrugged her shoulders and said nothing. She stood in the middle of the room, with her back to me.

"Look, it's only natural for me to be cautious," I said. "I don't know what to expect. I mean, Jim Otis could have been in the back, keeping you covered. It's not as if I suspected you of anything."

"You didn't ?" she asked without turning.

"Of course not," I said, trying to sound completely sincere. Inside, I felt wretchedly ashamed that, of course, I *had* suspected exactly that.

"Did you think I'd try to get you to kiss me if'n it meant that you was gonna get your head shot off?" she asked.

"No . . . I . . . I guess I just wasn't thinking."

Her back remained turned to me, but her shoulders were not quite as stiff. She seemed almost ready to accept that as an explanation, not because it was any good as an explanation, but just because she wanted not to be angry any longer.

I couldn't think of anything more to add. So I waited, and finally she turned and said, "Okay, well, you can kiss me now."

I went over and put my arms around her. She kissed me, and clung to me long enough so that I could begin to feel the warmth of her body permeating the chill of mine. Then she pulled away.

"You'd best wash up for dinner," she said. "There's hot water in the kettle."

I obeyed, splashing the hot water into the basin, taking off my shirt, and scrubbing my face and neck, hands and forearms. Then I sat down at the table and watched her serve up two steaming bowls of stew.

She did not seem at all surprised to have me back. But I felt sure that she would have accepted it with as much equanimity if I had stayed out in the hills, stalking Jim Otis, for a week, or until the job was done; or even if I had gotten killed and never come back. I don't mean to suggest that there was any implication in her manner that I ought to have stayed out in the hills until the job was done, or that it didn't matter to her whether I came back or not. In fact, it was just the opposite of that—I don't think I'd ever felt so welcome anywhere.

Not much had been changed in the cabin, and yet everything was different. There were curtains flanking the windows—flour-sack curtains, to be sure, but curtains nonetheless. A whiskey jug had become a vase for flowers in the center of the table. The old greasy rug that covered the trap door had been taken out and beaten, without doubt the only beating it had received since it had been brought to the cabin, and it actually looked like a rug again. You could tell, for the first time, that it was green.

"Why is Jim Otis doing all this?" I asked her.

She shrugged. "He's just crazy, I guess. I dunno, it just seems like something he's gotta do."

"Like killing Leona? Was that something he had to do?"

She did not reply.

"How come you and he never got together?" I asked.

"I didn't want Jim Otis Churchwarden for my man," she said.

"There must be more to it than that. You hid him from the law," I said. "You did let him stay at your place in Waynesville—he wasn't forcing you."

It was half a question, still, even though I stated it flatly. She nodded agreement.

"Why, after what he did to your sister?"

"He was Leona's man. She chose him. Leona knew what sort of man she was gettin' when she married Jim Otis—least, most ways she did."

"She was only thirteen!"

She shrugged.

"How much could she have known?"

"Much as you can know, before you do it, that is. An' he knew what he was gettin' in her."

"But he killed her. And she was only thirteen."

"Some folks is meant to live longer'n others, I guess. My sister Willa died when she was a week old, an' my sister Bonnie died when she was six months old. I had a brother died 'fore he ever had a name."

"Why did you hide Jim Otis out?"

"He come to me. If you don't know, I can't explain."

I didn't know. Family loyalty? It seemed like just the opposite of that to me, unless it was some concept of family that I just wasn't tuned in to.

Well, I guessed it didn't matter. "I'm going to bed," I said. "I've got to get some rest, so I can get up early tomorrow and figure out what I'm going to do."

She followed me into the bedroom.

I lit the hurricane lantern by the bedside. She reached over to blow it out. Without premeditation, I took her by the wrist and made her pause. She looked up at me, and I shook my head.

She accepted the command, and left the light on. She sat down on the bed beside me, looked at me and then averted her gaze.

She crossed her arms in front of her, grasped the opposite sides of her sweater in each hand, and worked it over her head. The she covered herself quickly again by folding up, leaning over double to unlace her boots.

She worked on her boots slowly and deliberately, loosening the laces one eyelet at a time, while I looked down at her broad back and counted the three hook-and-eye fasteners on her back—but resisted, for the moment, the temptation to start doing them.

Eventually both boots were off, and she straightened up again and faced me for just a second, her eyes shy but eager. Then she looked over hopefully at the light, then back to me again; but I would not change my mind, and she sat staring straight ahead of her, down at a spot on the floor just in front of her feet, her hands folded in her lap.

She wore a schoolgirl's bra, plain white cotton with a pink ribbon at the center of it. Leaning forward gave her a little roll of fat at the waist, which protruded over blue jeans that were stiff and bulky at the top, then tapered down to narrow legs that ended about two inches above her ankle, or roughly where her white socks began.

I slid around to kneel on one knee on front of her, and unsnap the front of her jeans. She made no move to resist, but her body stayed stiff and unsensual, and she continued to look wistfully at the light. But I was not going to blow it out. Damn it, I wanted to see her! This fifteen-year-old mountain mistress of mine, I wanted to see what she looked like.

I took off her socks, then grasped both of her hands in mine, and pulled her to her feet. She came up heavily, like a dead weight, but she kept her balance when I let go of her hands, though her shoulders sagged. I unzipped her fly and peeled her jeans down past her hips. She mechanically lifted one foot and then the other, at my prodding. The same, next, with her pink underpants with the frayed waist band.

I rocked back on my heels to look up at her.

From the bottom up: her legs were flawless, perfectly shaped with an easy rippling muscle tone, and pale, sexy thighs blending into blond hair that began as fuzz and grew thicker, but still silky and gentle, at the center. There was not much curvature in her hips yet; they were still a girl's. Her waist was broad, but the broadness was much too firm to be called flab; and her belly was almost flat.

I started to reach up and unhook her bra, but she did that herself, reaching up behind her back. Her shoulders made three quick jerks, one for each hook, and then they curved forward and down to let the straps slide off.

Her breasts were large, and plump, but not round yet. They looked as if they were still rising and filling out, like yeast dough; and the nipples had no color in them yet, there was no contrast between them and her breasts.

In fact, her whole body seemed like a photographic print of a perfect plump nude, still floating in the developer tray in a darkroom.

I almost felt that if I stared at it long enough, it would develop before my eyes: the breasts round out, the hips and waist develop their contours, the nipples their contrast.

She stood there, on uneasy but acquiescent display, until I blew out the lamp. Then she got under the covers, and I undressed and joined her.

Her body came alive when we touched, and she pressed it against mine, rubbing up and down, back and forth. It was an unlearned, undirected ardor born more out of a desire to please, and an eagerness to *do it*, than out of any real sense of how to get the most pleasure from her activity.

The not-quite-formed, still-developing beauty of her body still glowed in my vision. Her incredible youngness shot through me like a current. It was no longer something I wanted to forget—now it excited me immeasurably, and I wanted to focus her body on the pleasure it could enjoy.

I started by kissing her throat and the hollow of her breastbone. She gasped, and she gasped again as I ran my tongue along that cleft between her breasts.

There were more gasps, and cooing sounds, as I worked my way down her body; but when I reached her clitoris, there was a startled "oh!" and then silence.

She was holding her breath, and I could feel tremors beginning somewhere within her. I clasped her ass in both hands, pulled her tightly against my mouth, stuck my tongue as deep into her as it would stretch, till my jaw ached from the strain, and held on fast as the spasms started coming. Only when my own answering spasms could be put off no longer did I relax the lock of my own mouth on her sex. I fairly leaped up her body, slid in between her thighs, and we locked together again.

"I didn't know . . . I never heard of that before!" she sighed, afterwards. "Do you . . . have you ever done it before? Do people really do that?"

"Yes," I said, amused, but in my own way just as thrilled as she was.

"Oh . . . oh, I can't believe it," she said. "It's so good . . . I never even heard of it before." She was silent and meditative for a few moments. "Well . . . I heard somethin' once about how boys would want you to do somethin' like that to them, but I never quite believed it. It sounded . . . I dunno, kinda yucky. But I guess it's not."

"No."

"And I never dreamed a girl could have it done to her."

"Well, now you see."

"Do you like to have it done to you?"

"Sure."

"I'll do 'er then," she said. "Tomorrow. . . ."

She cuddled up with her head on my chest, and closed her eyes. I don't know which of us fell asleep first.

She was up first, though, as usual. I woke happily, and lay in bed dreamily listening to the sounds of Carolee bustling about in the kitchen, but I remembered Jim Otis, and I sat upright as dread hit me, head on.

I got dressed, including my boots, and came out for breakfast. Carolee looked at the haunted expression in my eyes, and said nothing to me. She put my coffee and grits on the table, and then stood back.

I ate aimlessly, trying to focus my mind on a plan. It was no use. Everything dissipated itself in that cloud of dread and confusion, and I sank further and further into hopelessness. Carolee remained quiet and invisible the whole time, but after she had poured me a second cup of coffee, she spoke timidly.

"Ry . . ."

"Mm?"

"Do you think I'm pretty?"

"Mm-humm."

"I guess you've seen lots of girls in the city . . . like . . . like last night."

I looked at her. "You're prettier than any of them."

Then I turned my thoughts back to my troubles, and she became the patient country wife again, and shut up.

I went up to the still. It seemed like as good a spot as any to start looking for clues. Jim Otis might have visited it during the night. Once a moonshiner, always a moonshiner.

Sure enough, there in the soft ground around the ashes were what appeared to be fresh bootprints. And under a clump of bushes nearby, I spotted, uncorked and lying on its side, an earthenware jug. There was still a damp spot on the ground under it.

So he had been here! And recently; and he'd left drunk, from the looks of it: that carelessly abandoned, half-empty jug, and the broken limbs of bushes and trampled foliage behind it—that had to be where he'd run off into the woods.

If he didn't sober up too quickly, he might not be hard to track. And if he didn't sober up at all, he might pass out on the trail up ahead. I wished I had a pair of handcuffs with me.

There was very little difficulty involved in tracking him through the woods. Even when I got to a stream it wasn't so hard. He had waded some distance along the stream bed to try and throw me off, but I reasoned that if he was drunk, he'd have been more likely to go downstream. Wading with the current would probably be a whole lot easier for a man in his condition.

Downstream it was, then. And I was right. About two hundred feet from where the trail had led into the water, there was a muddy, chewed-up patch of grass on the far bank. That would have to be where he had scrambled out.

Only a couple of hundred yards: not a very good attempt at evasiveness. I guessed that slogging through the water must have gotten too hard for him—I'd even had trouble keeping my balance a couple of times. Well, all I could hope was that falling down in the cold water hadn't sobered him up too much.

I was soon proved right in my conjecture about where he'd left the stream. And perhaps right about his starting to sober up, too. The trail was still there, but it was not quite so easy to follow. He was getting less clumsy.

At the same time, the underbrush was getting thicker. No trails seemed to crisscross this section of the woods, just thicket and bramble that grew thornier and denser the deeper I went into it. It was miserable going: my boots still squished from the stream, and my wet socks were making my feet start to blister. Thorny branches seemed to whip around from nowhere to scratch at my hands and face and tear my clothes. Vines and roots found ways to wrap themwhere to scratch at my hands and face and tear my only consolation was that the same thickness of the underbrush made Jim Otis' trail still possible to follow, although he was getting cleverer. There was no way that anyone could have gotten through that tangle without leaving trampled skunk cabbages, torn vines, smeared ground cherries, cracked branches, even an occasional snarl of threads from a snagged garment.

The sun was high overhead, and hot, since there was not much in the way of tall trees where I was walking, just secondary growth. It dried up my soaking trouser legs, but it just made my feet the more uncomfortable; and it was making me sweat heavily, too, which probably attracted even more insects than there would have been otherwise, if that was possible. Mosquitoes, midges, blackflies—they settled on me and stole my blood, they made clouds in front of my eyes, blundered into my ears and nose, and were sucked halfway down my throat when I gasped for breath.

Still I followed Jim Otis. My gun was starting to feel very heavy. I carried no other supplies except for ammunition, a canteen, and some jerky in my pocket—with Carolee to go back to, and the cabin, I could afford to travel light. I wondered what Jim Otis was carrying.

Then I lost the trail.

It just suddenly petered out. I retraced my steps to the last sign I had been able to identify clearly, and cast around for a new direction to pick it up in, as I had done several times before.

But this time there was nothing. The trail I had been following led along a ridge, below which was a steep embankment of dirt and shale and loose rock, with another, denser thicket in the gully below. It was too steep and treacherous to climb down. To the other side of the trail, there were more of the same scrub cedars and bramblebushes I had been going through, stretching away up hill to where the soil changed, or something, and it became more of a real forest again. I made several forays into the brush, in different directions, but each time I came up with nothing.

So I had lost him.

Unless he had gone down the embankment. It was crazy, but it was the only possible choice left. I looked up and down the length of the ridge, and sure enough, no more than twenty feet from where I had lost the trail, I found it again.

There was a part of the lip of the embankment that seemed to have crumbled away somewhat more, or somewhat more recently, than the rest. I looked down, and sure enough, for the forty-odd feet down to the thicket, there was scuffed-up dirt, signs of shale slide, overturned rocks with their dark, moist, soil-covered side up. And at the bottom, broken branches that indicated the spot where somebody had lurched into the thicket.

I guessed that had to be the way down, precarious though it would be. I wondered what would be the way up.

I wondered, too, if this could be the end of the chase. If Jim Otis was waiting in that thicket down there, I'd make an easy target, scrambling down that long, exposed open space. I hadn't seen any evidence up until now that he'd been doing anything but fleeing; still, he'd have to stop and make a stand somewhere, wouldn't he? That was what this whole hunt was about.

I backed off from the ledge a few paces, lay down on my stomach, and peered over the edge. I didn't expect to see anything then and there, but maybe if I waited quietly, there would be some telltale sign, a sound or a movement.

There was nothing. I can't say how much time went by. Certainly more than half an hour, probably more than an hour. Finally, I decided I'd have to risk it. If he was well inside the thicket, he'd have to come back out to get a clear shot. Besides, I'd be moving pretty fast and pretty erratically, so I'd have a fair chance of making it down without being hit, if it came to that.

And it might not—I didn't know what kind of shape Jim Otis was in, down there. He might have fallen—he might well be lying back in the thicket, too badly hurt to move. It was a long, treacherous way down.

I swung over the side quickly, and gave myself up to gravity, trying to steer my course and control the speed of my descent with one hand and my feet, while holding tightly to my rifle with the other hand.

The embankment was even more treacherous than I had imagined, and I cursed Jim Otis as the ground crumbled away beneath me: rocks uprooted themselves and failed to break my plummeting fall, and the sharp, flat pieces of shale sliced at my legs.

Then I felt my ankle turn under me. I threw up my hands, and my rifle flew out of my grasp and slid away on its own path. I continued to career wildly down the rest of the way, defenseless, in pain and panic.

But there seemed to be no ambush waiting for me. At least, not so far. I rolled over, not yet daring to try and get to my feet, and looked for my rifle.

It was stuck on the hillside, some fifteen feet above

me. I looked up at it, feeling the throbbing begin in my ankle. There was no way I would be able to climb back up to it. I would have to try to dislodge it, and make it slide down.

There was plenty of debris near me. I picked up a good-sized stone and threw it at the rifle. My first throw missed, and so did my second. The third try moved it slightly, down a few feet. Now it rested on a pile of loose shale. One properly placed rock should start the whole mass moving; but in fact, it took four more before I hit the mark.

Then everything happened with tremendous speed. My gun came sliding down at me, and half the hillside with it. I tried to spring back out of the way, but I had forgotten my ankle. It gave under my weight, and I went down heavily on my back. I threw one arm up in front of my face, but a sharp rock got past it. I ducked, but not quite fast enough. The rock glanced off my arm and struck me in the temple.

I was only dazed for a few moments, but blood was running freely down the side of my face. I had to tear my undershirt in half, to use one piece to mop away the blood from my brow, cheek, and jaw, and the other for a bandage.

My rifle lay only a few yards from me. I had succeeded in that, at least. I crawled over to it, and using it as a cane, pulled my self to my feet.

I tried to take a step, but my ankle throbbed unmercifully, and I crumpled to the ground again. How was I possibly going to continue on the chase like this? There was no way. With short, painful steps, and leaning heavily on the butt of my rifle, I dragged myself over to the thicket and peered in.

That was as far as I needed to go. I could see it all from where I was standing. The trail of crushed bushes led only about ten or fifteen feet into the thicket, and at the end of it rested a large boulder.

There was no more chase to continue. Not here.

Jim Otis had rolled this rock off the ridge, down the embankment, for me to follow. Then he had slipped off into the woods, leaving no sign that I could recognize.

As he could have done, at any time. He had laid down an elaborate sucker trail for me and I had fallen for it, all the way down to the bottom of a cliff.

Now my ankle hurt far too much for me to walk on it. It was impossible, even if I could have walked, to go back the way I had come. I would have to rest, then find a different route. And dusk was coming on. It was going to be a long, cold night in the woods, and I had no bedroll and no blanket.

CHAPTER 11

The next morning, I was able to walk. My ankle wasn't as badly turned as it might have been; the pain had subsided a lot.

But it still hurt. And the rest of me was completely miserable. I had passed a fitful night, too weary to do anything but sleep, and too cold and uncomfortable to do that. So my entire night had been spent in a kind of alert coma, my mind not functioning except to tell me of some new physical torment that had arrived: my shirt had pulled out of my pants at the back, so that the cold wind was blowing right onto my bare skin; I was lying on a root that was dug into my rib cage; the cramp in my hip was getting so intolerable that I'd have to stretch out to relieve it, and that would make me lose what little body heat I'd gathered by lying curled up. And my body clung to immobility as if it were a substitute for sleep: I could never bring myself to shift position until I was only seconds away from screaming in agony.

I saw the sky start to grow gray, but somehow I missed the sunrise. It was daylight the next time I opened my eyes, but I still resisted getting up as long as I could, as though I expected that if I held out long enough, some merciful god would finally relent and give me a little real sleep.

Or perhaps it was knowing how much I would ache when I did start to move. I lurched to my feet and immediately felt a surge of dizziness so strong that it sent me back, reeling, onto my hands and knees. I got up again more slowly, holding my head as if I had a hangover.

My brain swam again, but this time I rode it out, and remained standing. Now I could feel the aching and stiffness in every one of my joints and the tenderness that still afflicted my ankle; and I was weak from fatigue and hunger. But there was no help for any of these conditions in staying where I was, so I started right off to try to make my way back.

Getting back to the cabin took all of that day, with frequent stops to rest my ankle combined with getting lost half a dozen times, and it was dark again by the time I got there.

I was practically beside myself with joy when I saw the cabin, but I cautioned myself not to do anything rash, not to take the chance of getting caught off guard. I started to approach the building slowly and warily, holding my rifle out in front of me.

That lasted about three steps. Then I broke into a headlong, wobbly run, burst through the door of the cabin, said something to Carolee that was either a strangled cry or just a groan, I have no idea which, and collapsed flat on my face.

I regained consciousness on top of the bed. I was in my underwear, and I felt warm and damp.

As my perceptions became more formed, I realized that Carolee was sitting beside me, with a basin of hot water and a cloth, cleaning my wounds and scratches, gently washing off the caked blood. I moaned, opened my eyes, and smiled at her. She smiled back, and I reached up and held her hand as she dabbed at my neck and shoulder. She let the smile linger for a moment longer, gazing down at me; then she gently withdrew her hand from mine and soaked the cloth again in the hot water.

She worked on me quietly and with dedication. The fuzziness and the worst of the discomfort left me, gradually, and I began to be able to enjoy it.

The water was starting to cool off, and she went to get some more from the stove. I lay back contentedly and waited for her return.

"Do you roll over, I'll start on your back," she said when she got back. I obediently rolled over onto my stomach, marveling at how good I was starting to feel, considering how many parts of my body still hurt.

"How long was I out?" I asked.

"Not long. Half hour, maybe," she said, applying the cloth to my shoulder blade.

"It's still evening, then. Ohh . . . oww! I guess I'm all in one piece, though. At least, with you to patch me up I am."

She didn't say anything, but I could tell she was pleased. Her fingertips communicated it.

"Were you worried when I didn't come home last night?"

"Mm-mm."

"You weren't afraid Jim Otis had gotten me?"

I was a little disappointed that she hadn't been worried about me, but at the same time proud that she'd had enough confidence in me not to worry.

"No. Jim Otis was here yesterday."

"*What?*"

I rose up on my elbow, and stiffened in disbelief. I was so shocked that I didn't even notice at first how badly skinned my left elbow was, and the pain didn't register on me until it was so intense that my body just buckled, and I fell flat on my face.

"Jim Otis was here?"

"He come by yesterday afternoon. Said he'd laid a false trail for you and you was off in the woods follerin' it, so I knowed you was all right. I didn't worry none."

"But . . . that's not the point! How could you let him in here? How could you spend the afternoon just calmly talking to Jim Otis? Don't you know what's going on? Don't you know what he's trying to do to me?"

She nodded.

I sputtered. "Don't you know what he's trying to do?" I repeated, frustrated.

"He ain't gonna do it in here."

"Oh, yeah? What makes you so sure? What? What?"

She just shook her head and spoke with that absolute assurance that I recognized in her voice by now, but never understood.

"He ain't gonna. He ain't gonna do no fightin' an'

shootin' in my house, 'gainst my man. I ain't gonna stand for it. That's all there is to that."

"That's the whole point, Carolee! If you're not just playing house, if I really do mean something to you, where's your sense of— That man is a maniac! He's trying to kill me!"

"That's you and him's business. It's between you an' him, an' it's men's business. I don't want nothin' to do with it. If it was up to me, you wouldn't be goin' out there at all."

"Carolee, it's not a game. You have to take a side."

"If it's not a game, why do I have to take a side? I thought it was games as you had to choose up sides for."

"But you're involved, too!"

She shook her head firmly. "It's men's business, that shootin' an' killin' an' fightin'."

"And if he had killed me, would you have invited him in then, too? If he'd killed your man?"

"He killed my sister."

Now I was outraged at her for that, too.

"What kind of woman are you? What kind of a girl— a woman—whatever, what kind of a person are you? How can you—"

"Just do what it's my place to do, like everyone else," she said. "You an' Jim Otis, too. Don't matter none to me what you do out there. I'll have a hot meal on the stove an' a warm bed for you when you come back."

"Oh, and is that what you gave Jim Otis, too? Equal time, equal hot meal, equal warm bed? Is that your game?"

"Boy, you don't know nothin', do you?" she said. She turned away from me, half sulking, half blazing. I was angrier than ever. What right did she have to make me feel I was going too far?

"Did he tell you he'd fixed it so I wouldn't get home all night? Did you both figure you'd be safe, with me lying out under a bramblebush someplace, freezing and cut up and with a sprained ankle? When did he leave? This morning? This afternoon?"

"You don't know what you're talkin' about," she said. "He left last evenin'. After supper. I fed him supper." Her voice was weary. "You're bein' an awful blamed fool."

I went out into the other room. She didn't follow me. The chill of the night air seemed to find its way into the front room even more keenly than to the bedroom, in spite of its being closer to the stove. I started to unroll a blanket and make myself a pallet on the floor.

"Come on to bed an' don't be no more foolish than you need to be," came Carolee's voice from the bedroom.

"No," I said thickly, trying not to feel foolish.

I waited for her to say something more, but there was only silence from the bedroom. I settled down on my pallet to try and sleep.

I was too angry to sleep, and too tired not to. I remember lying down, my body tense and my eyes wide open, but I don't remember much more.

I didn't want to see Carolee in the morning. I wanted to wake up earlier than she did, and get ready to go, and be gone. But, of course, it didn't turn out that way. The smell of the hotcakes cooking and coffee brewing on the stove were what woke me, and I realized that it was already full daylight.

Everything was turning against me, even my will. Nothing was working out the way I wanted it to. Panic took hold of me, and made me clumsy. I stumbled past the table, knocking over a chair. I tried to get around Carolee, but she stood her ground.

"I'll fix my own breakfast," I said.

"You'll get out of my kitchen," she said. "If there's any breakfast fixin' here, I'll be fixin' it."

I wanted to turn on my heel and walk out of the cabin. But I needed the coffee, and the smell of the hotcakes reminded me forcibly that I was just too hungry to turn my back on them for a principle. I spun around abruptly, made a motion to stalk out, but ended up sitting meekly at the table.

I walked aimlessly for about half an hour. At first I felt completely cut off, adrift, alone, confused. Birds twittered in the trees above my head, and a rabbit ran across my trail. I heard and saw it all, just as if I had nothing more pressing to concentrate on.

But as I walked, my mind started to clear. I could feel it clearing just as though I was watching something out in front of me, as though it were a pond that had been churned and muddied up, and now all the silt was gradually settling again.

I was really alone now—nothing and nobody to look out for but myself. I'd left Carolee behind, and I wasn't going back.

Well, that was what I wanted—what did any of this

mean to me, this cabin, these hillbillies? I was a U.S. marshal from Washington, D.C., and nothing that went on here had anything to do with my life or my values, only with my duties as a peace officer.

What was I doing playing cowboys and Indians, running around the mountains with a gun in my hand, waiting for a maniac to ambush me? What had happened to my common sense? What had happened to my *training*?

There was only one thing to do—and I couldn't believe that I hadn't thought of it earlier. I couldn't believe that it hadn't been my first thought; I must have been bewitched.

I had to get out of here. It was that simple. I had to get back to town and contact the state police. With a troop of men, and a couple of helicopters, and maybe some dogs, they could flush Jim Otis out right away.

The route back wasn't hard to retrace, and walking it was a pleasure. I hardly felt sore at all, as I briskly followed the trails that Jim Otis had led us up. I was trying to decide how my story would sound in the papers—heroic or ridiculous. If I told it right, it ought to be heroic—especially if I ended up by catching Jim Otis, or even leading the authorities to him. I was sure Captain Falkner would want me to go along in one of the helicopters and point out the trail, and maybe even be there when they nabbed him, even though it wasn't exactly in my jurisdiction.

I passed by the weird old ruined mansion. I was definitely on the right track, and the crumbling building seemed like a gateway now, between craziness and sanity. And this time, I was going through it the right way.

I wondered if there was any way I could get my car unstuck from where Jim Otis had left it. It was pretty well jammed in there, as I remembered it; but if I rocked it, and maybe dug out around the wheels enough for it to get some traction, it might be possible. I wondered how far out into the country the telephone lines came—how far I'd have to go before I could call for help.

With luck, I'd have a posse up before nightfall. By tomorrow morning for sure, the helicopters would be out, the dogs would be sniffing through the woods, and we'd have him treed like a coon— How do you like that, hey, Cousin Jim Otis?

By now I was coming down into the ravine that went alongside of the rapids, and I was starting to feel just a little fatigue again. Right up ahead of me, I knew, was that narrow ledge that I'd had such a close call negotiating on the way up. Jim Otis had saved my life then, not that I felt any obligation or gratitude to him at this point. But I'd have to be extra careful negotiating it on the way out, because I'd be all alone. So it was no time to start running out of steam.

I was still carrying the rifle. Well, it was excess baggage now. I wasn't going to be able to make that leap up onto the ledge carrying anything so big in one hand. And I had no intention of wasting any more time hunting Jim Otis, so there was no point tiring myself lugging its weight around. I felt funny about parting with it, though. Not because I needed it, so much as . . .

I caught myself. And I was furious with myself. Sentimental about Jim Otis Churchwarden, even now? I raised the rifle over my head, and hurled it far into the bushes.

Another forty minutes' walk brought me to the flat rock that I had slid off, the one with the narrow ledge at the other side of it.

I stopped and looked at it, and a wave of fear passed over me. I remembered Jim Otis racing down that rock and leaping up to the ledge. It had all happened so fast, then, that I hadn't stopped to think about how he had done it. Instinct, adrenaline, luck— for me, now, with time to think about it, it was a hell of a dangerous jump, and I didn't see how I was going to do it. Especially with the memory of that terror in the rapids to inhibit me.

I had the memory of that terror in the mountains to spur me on, though. I'd make the leap. I had to.

If they caught Jim Otis, it would be a real feather in my cap around the department. I might even get a special citation for it. That would be funny: a special citation for valor, because I had enough sense to turn around and go for help.

But that was what police work was all about, not playing cowboys. Not playing the games that Jim Otis had tried to sucker me into.

I was ready to make the leap. I paced it once, being very careful of my footing all the way down the rock and all the way back up. In fact, I came back up on all fours, concentrating to keep out the panic.

At the top of the rock, I straightened up and took a

deep breath. Then a small chunk of stone next to me leaped into the air.

I looked down, startled, not sure that I had seen right. Then it happened again.

I knew what it was. I knew, even though the roar of the rapids made it impossible to hear the crack of a rifle fired from the cliffs on the other bank.

I slid off the rock in a hurry, and huddled down behind it. That was the end of my escape plan. I was a shooting-gallery target, if I tried to creep along that ledge with Jim Otis taking dead aim at me. I was going to have to retreat.

Another bullet whistled over my head, just to let me know he was still there. And while I knew it was impossible, since I hadn't even been able to hear his gunshots over the rapids, I still could have sworn I heard laughter.

So it was back up the trail again. I couldn't stay where I was. That is—I could, and did, stay where I was for a long time, but that was fright, not strategy. I simply didn't dare to move.

But eventually I had to start back, still without any clear strategy in mind—only the knowledge that I couldn't sit behind that rock forever. But if I went back, maybe there'd be another trail, a safer one, more ambush-free. And maybe I'd find it.

Sure, that was it. Another way down the mountain. I knew there was one—Jim Otis had talked about it. All I had to do now was give Jim Otis the slip, and I had a pretty good head start on him. Then I'd find it, and I'd get down to civilization and Captain Falkner and a telephone and the helicopters.

I was sorry I'd been so impetuous with my gun. I still had no intention of making any kind of an attempt to stand and fight, but on the whole, it would be better to have it than not to. I'd have to search for it in the bushes—if I could remember what the place where I'd thrown it away looked like.

I was sure I'd be able to; but suddenly I started seeing familiar landmarks around every bend in the trail. Hadn't there been a dead tree that looked like that one, with the double fork in it? I had been standing next to a big rock with green and yellow lichens on it—hadn't I? A rock like this one? No, it had been by itself, and there were two rocks here. Unless I just hadn't noticed the other one. But I didn't remember any mossy overhang behind my back . . . but on the other hand, I couldn't remember what had been behind my back. How about up ahead there, that big bush, twenty feet back from the trail? Hadn't I thrown it into a big bush?

I left the trail and went down to check the bush, thrashing through it and walking around all sides. When I'd finished, I'd gotten nothing for my efforts except some new scratches and some grave doubts as to whether I *had* thrown it anywhere near a bush.

I kept walking, checking out this spot, dismissing that one, finding nothing. A couple of places I had passed over began to loom so large in my mind that I actually went back to look them over, only to have my original estimate of them reaffirmed.

There was no use trying to judge by time or distance—my pace and mental state were so different now from when I had come down, that neither could serve as a constant. I had to keep looking, by trial and error, through all the woods all up and down the trail. It seemed like a hopeless cause.

Then I found the gun. Finding it was even more nerve-shattering than looking for it fruitlessly had been.

It was propped up against a rock by the side of the path.

CHAPTER 12

The message was clear enough. Jim Otis wasn't tired of the game yet. He wasn't ready to quit, and he didn't want me to quit, either. More than that, he was going to make sure that I didn't. Like a bucket of water in the face during a barroom brawl—wake up, dummy, and get back in the fight.

That was frightening enough, but that was only the half of it. I realized, now, what kind of close surveillance I was really under. Jim Otis must have been trailing me the whole way. So that when I threw my gun into the bushes, he had retrieved it and left it for me to find when I came back. Then he had forded the rapids somehow, at some spot which he knew and I didn't, and waited on the opposite bank to head me off.

He was everywhere! And he had me in his sights all the time. And now . . . now he wanted to play with me a little longer, before he finished me off.

I almost did not even pick up the gun. For a minute I had a crazy impulse just to leave it there and run, screaming, up the trail, down the trail, into the woods—it didn't matter where—mad and defenseless, letting the whole responsibility slip out of my hands altogether. Then whatever happened, it wouldn't be my fault—even I got killed, it wouldn't be my fault, I wouldn't have had any part in it.

If I did pick up the gun, I might be shot, then and there. I no longer had any doubt but that Jim Otis was watching every move I made, every second of the day and night. I had no way of knowing which move might be the one that would set him off.

I edged over to the gun, stood beside it, and then quickly stooped and picked it up. I had intended to run for cover as soon as I had it in my hands, but instead I just stood there dumbly, holding the rifle up in front of me. My eyes were closed. I made my ears buzz, so I wouldn't hear the shot if it was fired. I didn't want to know about it.

But there was no shot, and I began to feel absurdly self-conscious, like a man who has just discovered there is a hidden TV camera on him. I started trying to act nonchalant. I posed, leaning on the barrel of the gun, looking thoughtful. I sat down on the rock and began to check the rifle over very carefully for possible damage, sighting down the barrel, going through the motions of adjusting the sight, checking the safety mechanisms.

I yawned; I stretched. I even sat down and ate, my first meal of the day, even though I was not at all hungry, and the food seemed so dry I choked on it. Then I pantomimed thinking about continuing on up the trail, but deciding instead that it was time to make camp for the night.

I tested the wind with a moistened finger in the air,

picked the leeward side of a clump of bushes, and opened up my bedroll. I lay down to sleep with my rifle across my chest.

The weather was starting to turn colder, and that night was a particularly chilly one. I woke with the first rays of dawn to see the evidence of a hard frost around me, and little clouds of breath in front of my face. I got up and started moving about immediately, to get my blood circulating again, and so that I wouldn't have too much time to reflect on what I was doing and get self-conscious again.

But it was impossible not to think about being watched. It preyed on me with every step I took; I felt like a specimen swimming on a slide under a microscope.

"*Come on and show yourself!*" I screamed at last. "*Shoot me, face me! Coward! Do something!*"

But I got only an echo for an answer.

How long would he stalk me? I saw the glint of a gun barrel in every tree. Twice I fired at movements in the bushes; that just made more of an echo than the shouting. I thought I would never stop hearing it reverberate through the woods.

An echo is a lonely sound; you shouldn't have to hear it when somebody else is close by. Jim Otis should have absorbed some of that sound for me, but he didn't. I just went on and on. . . .

Suddenly, I came upon the clearing with the ruined mansion. I stood and stared at it, confused—then I didn't have to go through the gorge to get to the mansion! That had just been another part of Jim Otis' false trail in bringing me up.

Well, it had worked. I couldn't have been more turned around if he'd brought me blindfolded. I crossed the clearing and stood near the house. Was there another way out of here? Or should I go back to the cabin? If it came to a seige, I'd have more food and supplies there than he would. Maybe I could hold out, force a showdown that way.

I couldn't go back to the cabin, and Carolee. I wouldn't.

Then the shot came.

It came from behind me. It whistled past my shoulder, and bored a hole in one of the Greek-style columns that flanked the front door of the house, taking a lot of the crumbling, rotten wood with it. I bolted, and ducked inside the house just as I heard a second shot.

I had a fairly good idea of the direction the two shots had come from. I leaned around the corner of the upper door and fired an exploratory shot back. It was answered immediately, and I ducked back as the bullet hit the half-open front door and made a splintering sound.

I'd been fairly close to the target. Maybe eight to ten feet to the left of where the last shot had come from. I pumped off two more quick ones at the spot, and ducked back into the house.

I sped for a window as two more shots pounded the door, and got there fast enough to see a puff of smoke; I fired back at it. He answered with a shot through the window, and even though I had to duck away quickly again, I could tell that his shot had come from the same place as the last one.

He wasn't moving around, then. That was good and bad. He must have pretty good cover where he was, but at least I'd have his location pegged, for whatever good it might do me.

At least there was something to fight against now, some action and an opponent that I could locate. I could never have imagined that being shot at could feel so reassuring.

I fired another volley through the window, just to make sure we were still communicating, and got a barrage of shots in return, one of which was so close it made me wince. I moved back about six feet from the window.

Backing up, I missed seeing a rotten floorboard, and suddenly I went through the floor and fell heavily. I toppled backward, and my rifle went off next to my ear. I had nearly blown my own head off.

I didn't seem to have hurt myself, but I stood for a moment with my foot still sticking through the hole in the floor and reflected on my chances. Maybe that was the answer, I thought wryly: if all else fails, I could kill myself and spoil Jim Otis' fun. It was a grisly thought, and I decided to drop it. I certainly wasn't much pleased with the idea of doing it accidentally.

As long as we were trading shots, I still had a pretty good chance. But if I was going to be moving around, I needed to check my fortress out more closely.

The floors were pretty rotten all over, but some of the boards seemed more decrepit than others. If I could make allowances for them and try to stay on the joists as much as possible, I should have a fair amount of mobility.

The house did not look like any abandoned building I had ever seen before. That was partly because it was a mansion, and partly because it hadn't been vandalized. Everything that had been left behind was still just where it had been left, settling into decay with the walls and floorboards.

I was in the front hall, but I could see partway through the parlor and the kitchen. The kitchen had a huge cast-iron stove, an old wood-burning stove standing on claw-shaped legs, with incredible ornamental curlicue designs all over it. There wasn't much question as to why it had been left behind—the thing must have weighed close to a quarter of a ton. I wondered what it would be worth to an antique dealer, if you could get it out and take it back into town. It was tilted at a sharp angle, going downward toward the side I couldn't see through the doorway. The legs on the other side must have either broken or gone through the floor.

I was starting to feel the urge to do some more shooting. I tiptoed over to the window I had used before, and aimed a shot at the place in the woods I had been aiming at. An answering shot came back; so he hadn't moved yet.

There was nothing in the hall but a hat rack, and a hall table next to the banistered stairway. The table had once been furnished with a silver tray to hold calling cards, I supposed—though I couldn't imagine that very many people could have come calling up here. There were no other windows in the hall, though, so I squeezed off a couple more shots to keep Jim Otis honest, and made a careful dash for the parlor.

I had to climb up on the keyboard of an upright piano to get to the window. The keys squished down without making a sound, other than the thud of being depressed all the way; and when I moved off them, they did not come back up.

I fired again, but the angle was no better. I still could not see where I was shooting. The novelty of the gunplay was wearing off, and I was starting to feel frustrated. And trapped. As long as I kept firing, there was a possibility of connecting with a lucky shot; but I knew it wasn't very likely. Jim Otis would be too well protected. And if I kept this up long enough, there was a certainty of my running out of ammunition, although I still had the better part of a box of fifty cartridges in my pocket. Good thing I hadn't thrown them out with the rifle.

How was I going to maneuver into a better position? There weren't many more windows downstairs, and none that seemed to have a better angle than any of the others. That left only one choice: upstairs. It might give me a new angle that would be better than anything I could get from down here. And he certainly wouldn't be expecting it.

I wasn't so sure I expected it of myself, either. I climbed down from the piano, walked back to the parlor door, and took a look at the staircase. It was rickety now, but it had once been sturdy enough. And if I kept to the inside close to the wall, the support might be stronger.

I had to try it. I engaged the safety on my rifle, and started up.

There were ten steps up to the landing. They creaked and groaned horrendously, but they held. My nervous imagination had Jim Otis hearing every creak from his hiding place out in the woods, but my common sense told me that was impossible.

The landing would take about two strides, possibly two and a half. I wished there were some way around it. I would have liked to leap over it, but I knew the steps above would not take that kind of pounding. So, still hugging the wall, I stepped gingerly out onto it.

The first step out was all right, but as I leaned into the second, I felt the flooring begin to give way. Fighting panic and an impulse to push off and make a leap for it, I tossed my gun onto the stair in front of me, and dropped to my hands and knees, equalizing my weight.

It worked. The landing sagged, but the boards didn't break; and I was still halfway to the upper floor. For several long moments I was too paralyzed to go any farther, but finally I was able to begin again, shuffling forward on my hands and knees. I climbed the first two steps after the landing on my knees, then straightened up and walked the last three as I'd walked the first flight, clinging to the wall.

The upstairs floor sagged like a cheap mattress, and my heart sank as far as the center of the flooring when I first saw it. I couldn't imagine those floorboards supporting me all the way over to the window. No way in the world . . . but I had to try it. I didn't have any other, better chances for survival that I could think of. And I had to do it quickly, before Jim Otis got the idea that I was up to something, and moved from his hiding place. If he came in downstairs while I was upstairs, I'd really be trapped.

I got down on my hands and knees again, pushing my rifle along in front of me, and moved toward the window as fast as I could, sliding, crawling, and shuffling; staying as far away from that sagging center as possible. Halfway across I developed an irrational fear that the angle of the sag was so steep that my gun would slide away from me and down into the center if I didn't hold it tightly. I couldn't shake the fear out of my mind, and I ended up clutching the rifle in one hand, and clumping along awkwardly, holding it out in front of me and skinning my knuckles when I tried to use that hand for balance, the rest of the way over.

I made it to the window, and peered out. It had worked! There was Jim Otis' shoulder and the side of his head, just where I had figured they ought to be. I rose up slowly on one knee, resting my rifle on the still and lining up Jim Otis in the sights.

I had never aimed a gun at a live human being before.

I paused just long enough for that one thought to pass across my mind, no longer; but it was time enough for Jim Otis to sense something, like the stag in the clearing. His head disappeared from sight just as I squeezed the trigger.

I missed. Jim Otis had ducked down behind the tree and was completely out of my field of vision. But that brief glimpse of him had triggered something inside me, too, and I couldn't stop. I just kept shooting and shooting.

Jim Otis fired back, and suddenly the air was full of bullets, as all of the pent-up frustration that came out of days on nonconfrontation, of stalking and being stalked, came blasting out in a torrent of gunfire. Nothing could make me stop pulling the trigger until finally the magazine was empty, and then I reloaded feverishly, with trembling fingers, fearful of losing any of the edge of my mania. It all felt like being in the middle of a war movie—as if there had to be more than just two people shooting at each other. The noise was deafening. It rocked the building.

I was so caught up in the frenzy of gunshots that I didn't notice it right away, but the building was taking a terrible beating from the barrage it was getting; perhaps from the shock of the sound waves, too. It was trembling, and it shuddered every time a bullet smashed into a beam.

Perhaps I had a sixth sense of danger, too, like Jim Otis and the stag. Or perhaps I had felt the house take an especially hard jolt, or maybe I heard something: I don't know. But I looked up at the ceiling just in time to see a large chunk of it cracking over my head, and I dived headlong across the room just as it fell in on the spot where I had been crouching.

Then a beam cracked. One end of it hit the floor with the force of a sledgehammer, shattering the floorboards and embedding itself in the hole it had created, so that the other end, when it tore loose from the ceiling, stuck up in the air like the prow of a sinking ship. I pressed up against the wall and watched as the reverberations from that crash seemed to strain the rest of the beams and rifle shots kept jolting the supports in the ceiling.

Another beam caved in. It crashed down inches from me, and I felt that the whole ceiling was just about ready to fall in on me and the whole floor was about to fall in under my feet. It looked as if the whole upper story of the building could go at any second.

I looked through the doorway next to me. There weren't any beams caved in yet in the bedroom, but plaster was falling from the walls and ceiling as though the whole house was being shaken.

I ran for the window, but I knew I was a long way from the ground. Too far to jump.

But right outside the window, I discovered, was that tree limb that had grown up against the side of the house and pushed it atilt. I could reach it with a leap from the window, and it looked as though it would probably hold me.

It would hold me. It might sway and bend a little, but it wasn't brittle like the house. Still, I held back. I'd have to drop my gun; I wouldn't be able to make a flying leap for a tree branch carrying it. And then I would be trapped. It would be the end of the line.

Maybe not, though. On the plus side, the house would be between me and Jim Otis. I'd be out of his line of vision, and perhaps before he realized what I was up to, I could crawl in as far as the main trunk of the tree, climb down, and make a run for it.

But I didn't like the odds on that, at all. There were too many variables piling up on top of one another, and each one leading me further into a trap. If I did make it down the tree, then what? I'd be in the worst trap of all. Running unarmed through the woods, being stalked by Jim Otis? Even if he didn't realize what I'd done right away and I was able to make it to the woods, he'd recover fast enough to pick up my trail.

I decided against it. I'd be better off to hang in there, somehow, and shoot it out. Maybe I could get one lucky shot in. It wasn't likely, but it was better than being chased like a rabbit through the woods.

Now beams were starting to crack in the room that I was in. I couldn't back up any further. And everything around me was trembling and shaking. I didn't know if I was imagining it or what, but the whole building seemed to be swaying, slipping. I panicked. I heaved my gun out of the window, and leaped for the tree.

I caught the branch with my arms, and with one foot just hooked over it. It bent down and snapped back, and I almost lost my grip. I slid halfway around it, but I managed to keep my calf and foot locked around the branch, so I was able to steady myself upside down, like a sloth, and then to throw my other leg over, and pull myself back up to the top.

I crawled a little farther along the limb, to where it was sturdier, and got up into a sitting position. Then I looked back at the house.

Its movement was slow and awesome. What was happening was unmistakable, but almost impossible to believe, even as I watched it. But it was happening. I could hear the groaning and tearing, the breaking up of rotted timbers. Gradually picking up speed as it went, the entire house was falling over on its side.

The smaller building, with nothing more to lean against, fell also. It clattered to the ground.

It was like watching an ocean liner sink, and very quickly it was over. Pieces of the columns protruded absurdly from under the rubble. They looked like victims, like the legs of victims of an enormous auto wreck. A few splintered, broken-off uprights were still standing, and part of a chimney, but everything else lay flattened.

And I was sitting in a tree in the middle of an empty clearing.

CHAPTER 13

Breaking the silence that had settled with the last echoes of the falling building, there came a hallooing cry from out beyond the clearing, from Jim Otis in the woods.

"Hey, Cousin Ry, whatcha doin' up in that tree?"

"You bastard!" I screamed at him. "You fucking psychopath, you murdering bastard! Are you going to shoot me from there, or are you going to come out and face me like a man to do it?"

It seemed like a dumb question as soon as I'd asked it. Even in my fear I was still capable of feeling self-conscious and dumb, especially while sitting up in a tree next to the remains of a collapsed mansion. Of course he'd come out—certainly Jim Otis, of all people, would not be squeamish about looking someone in the eye that he was about to kill.

"Not just yet, Cousin," came the answering call. "Set there awhile."

That was the last I heard. I waited for a few hours, until dusk, and then climbed down out of the tree. There was no shot, no sign of Jim Otis. I spent the night right there, at the foot of the tree.

I found my gun in the morning. It had been thrown clear of the falling building, and it lay near the tree, apart from the rubble. I picked it up mechanically. But it seemed like just another splintered board lying among the debris, for all the comfort I felt from it. I wasn't counting much on self-defense anymore. I wasn't counting much on anything. I didn't think there was anything that could help me.

I wandered in the woods for two days, hoping vaguely and wildly to stumble on some route back to civilization, fully expecting to be picked off as soon as I did find a route, expecting not to find a route at all.

Fear, desolation, the constant sense of being watched and mocked, though there was never a sign of another human being, made everything seem unreal and unnatural. The trees took on grotesque Satanic shapes, and I heard ghostly whispering in the leaves and underbush. I tried not to shout challenges into the air too often, because the silence mocked me after I did it; I tried not to talk to myself too much, because I took it as a sign that I was cracking up.

Cold, fatigue, and hunger were all real, and made their own strong bids for my attention. I was battered back and forth between the terrors of the unknown all around me, and the strain of all-too-concrete physical deprivation: so that when, toward evening of the second day, I saw a light through the trees, I asked myself not so much *whether* I was going crazy, as *how*—from which part of me the hallucination was coming.

But I went toward the light, anyway. And it turned out not to be a hallucination, although after I reached its source, I still wondered for a moment whether I might not be seeing things.

I had come upon a small, neat cabin, surrounded by a low white picket fence, standing by itself in the middle of the mountains. Between me and the cabin, sloping up to it, was a large plowed and tilled area—a garden, now mostly picked clean of the summer's crops, with the stalks and vines cut down and left in the fields to decay and fertilize the ground for next spring's planting. Beyond that, the picket fence, with a flower bed next to it. The gate was latched, though what it was expected to keep out or in, I couldn't imagine. Perhaps it was just that whoever lived there could not imagine a house without a picket fence, or a fence without a gate and latch.

Yes, it was really all there, right in front of me. And more than that, there was no way that it could have been whipped up overnight as a hoax by Jim Otis, like the trail into the thicket.

I walked up past the garden, lifted the latch on the gate, and went into the yard.

Two children came out on the porch to look at me. They were a girl and a boy. The girl was a teenager, the boy about eight. They were both blond and solemn-faced.

I didn't know if I could still manage to smile, and I didn't know if could talk to real people in a normal tone of voice, but I tried to do both.

"Hello," I said.

They didn't retreat screaming in terror, but they didn't answer me, either. They turned silently and went back into the house, closing the door behind them.

A new fear overtook me. These were people who lived alone, a long way from someone else. And they were hillbillies. The might shoot first and ask questions afterward—that happened, in these mountains. But I knocked at the door.

A woman answered.

She must have been the children's mother. I couldn't tell how old she was: certainly not young. Her face was unlined and her eyes were clear, but they had years in them. They looked at me with an expression that I understood to be welcome, though there was no smile to accompany it.

"May I come in?" I asked. "I'm afraid I'm lost, and I saw your cabin—"

"Come in," she said.

There was a table in the room, with chairs around it, and I took one of them, falling into it more than sitting, and resting my arms on the table. The teenage girl sat there, too, in a rocking chair across from me. She had a baby in her arms. The boy stood a short distance away. When his mother followed me back into the room and walked past the table to the kitchen stove, he moved close to her without exactly following her—it was more as if he were her moon, kept in her orbit by a natural gravitational pull. His eyes never left me.

Neither did the girl's. I hardly ever notice what color eyes people have, but these two children's were a striking clear gray; and as I looked at the two of them, it occurred to me that the mother's eyes were the same color.

Perhaps the color added something to the effect that their gaze had. It was direct, penetrating, and un-nerving. But completely polite. They were frankly cu-rious, but not hostile or inhospitable.

"I've been . . . all by myself in the woods for about four days," I said. I didn't know whether I should say anything about Jim Otis, and if so, what it should be, so I decided to just leave him out of it for the time being. "Really lost . . . don't know where I am . . . never expected to find a cabin back here."

"Have some tea," said the woman, putting a steam-ing cup in front of me. "I'm warming up some leftover stew for you, it will be ready presently." Her voice was low-pitched and gracious. It was all on one note, yet it was musical. It made me feel safe.

I took a sip of the tea. It tasted homemade, out of some mixture of mountain herbs. I felt stronger after the first sip—strong enough, at least, to talk without fearing that my voice would slide uncontrollably into a croak.

"My name's Ry Justice," I said.

"I am Rebekah Johnson," said the woman. "These be my children."

"Ephah," said the boy, offering me a sturdy hand-shake. "I'm pleased t' meet ye."

"My name is Shiphrah," said the girl. "It's from the Bible. Like his. The baby's name is Mizraim."

The baby had clear gray eyes, too. And even he had the look of knowing something I didn't know.

"I'm really lost," I said again. "I. . ."

"Don't try to talk till after ye've broken bread," she said. "To everything there is a season."

The girl held up the baby to her, and she took it in her arms. The daughter then got up from the rocking chair, and the woman took her place and began rocking slowly back and forth, holding the baby over her shoulder. A couple of times she glided over to stir the stew in the pot on the stove, and then moved back again, making it all one motion.

The woman sat and rocked, singing softly to her baby. It was an old Fundamentalist hymn she was crooning, I recognized that; but I did not remember which one. She made no concession to my presence, but she was never unaware of me. I was too tired, and too glad to be there—to be anywhere—for that to make me feel uncomfortable. I was never unaware of her, either, but the warmth of the stove, the relief of being able to sit in a chair, and the safety of indoors were enough to occupy my thoughts for right then.

The girl put a bowl of stew in front of me. I smelled it, and looked deep into the bowl. There were chunks of meat, and broth, and potatoes, and corn and black-eye peas. There was a pottery bowl, and a large soup spoon. I drank it all in with my eyes before picking up the spoon.

The first few bites were just to get some of the warmth and the sustenance inside me; then I began tasting it. It was delicious. Garden herbs gave it a delicate yet homespun flavor. The corn had apparently been pickled, and that added a sharpness to the taste that enhanced it terrifically. I ate slowly, and savored each bite.

"Do you live up here all by yourselves?" I asked Mrs. Johnson.

"No, I've got a man," she said. "He's gone t' town t' get some provisions. Flour, suchlike. We don't need much from town. He goes in every couple o' months."

"And what about you?"

"I stay up here. I ain't been off this mountain in five years."

"Five years? You mean you haven't been off it at all?" I asked incredulously.

"O Zion, that bringest good tidings, get thee up to the high mountain; O Jerusalem, that bringest good tidings, lift up thy voice with strength; lift it up, be not afraid; say unto the cities of Judah, behold your God!"

Her voice throbbed with warmth as she quoted. I guessed it had to be from the Bible.

"We used to live down in Dayton, Ohio," said Shiphrah, by way of explaining.

"I don't remember it at all," said the boy Ephah, with just a trace of pride—not so much that it could have been called a sin, I thought. His mother seemed to agree. Her eyes smiled at him.

"I do, but it don't hardly seem real no more," said Shiphrah. She pointed to the baby. "He's *never* been off the mountain."

"You don't come from the city, do you? You didn't just suddenly decide to—"

Mrs. Johnson shook her head. "My husband took us there so's he could work in a factory an' make money. He knows all about machines, he can do anything with them machines. But after three years I made him move back to the mountains."

"Mama had cancer," Shiphrah said, and an unmistakable note of pride crept into her voice, too. I was not sure why, until Mrs. Johnson went on to explain.

"Doctors gave me a year to live," she said. "So I came back here. 'I will lift up mine eyes unto the hills, from whence cometh my salvation.' I came back here and prayed. Took my cancer to the Lord, and he took it from me. Never been sick a day since."

"She cured Ephah, too," Shiphrah added.

I looked at the woman. She nodded. "When he was four, the pressure cooker blew up, and he was scalded. He was covered all over with second-degree burns. And the Lord healed him. I prayed to the Lord to heal him, and he did."

She pulled the boy's shirt back, exposing his neck and shoulder. There were the faint outlines of what had once been scars, but the skin looked whole and healthy.

She spoke without even that trace of pride that I had noticed in her children's voice, but without humility either—just a matter-of-fact acceptance of the close relationship between herself and miracles.

She rocked in silence, while I looked at her and thought about her story of curing herself. I could see no reason not to believe her.

"You came from the big house," she said. "The house as was destroyed and is no more."

Her face was not turned directly toward me, and she seemed to be mostly talking to herself; but I could tell that she was talking to me and looking at me.

"How did you know that?" I asked, flabbergasted.
"I saw it."

"You were there?"

"Mama has the gift," said Shiphrah.

"Second sight?"

"You contended there, and escaped with your life," she said. "But the house fell, and at last it is fallen forever."

"You know the house?" I asked stupidly.

The woman nodded. "It were my family's."

"Your family's!"

"My grandfather's father built it. I come from a very respectable family and a very old family."

"Pa built this house, though," said Ephah.

"If you know about the house, then you must know that I'm in very great danger," I said.

She rocked. I guessed that she knew.

"Do you know who Jim Otis Churchwarden is?"

"Yes, we know him."

"He's the one who's trying to kill me."

Mrs. Johnson was silent again, and I could tell that she was mulling it over. It did not seem to surprise her. Perhaps her second sight had told her that already, too.

I couldn't tell exactly what she was thinking. "I . . . I'm sorry about your house," I said. "I didn't mean to . . ."

"It was old and abandoned," she said. "It should have fallen a long time ago. It held all that was venal and sinful in my family. I never thought of it as my house. There was others in the family as did." Her face suddenly froze, hard. Once again, I didn't know what unspoken thought had caused it.

"Mama's great-granddaddy was rich," broke in Ephah.

"But his daughter turned her back on his wealth and married in the sight of the Lord," said Shiphrah, from memory, but not without conviction.

I suddenly thought of Carolee. What was she doing now? Was she still in the cabin? And who was there to take care of her now? No wonder her home came first with her.

"My great-grandfather was a proud man, but he was humbled," said Mrs. Johnson. "Money is the root of all evil."

"That's why we moved away from the city, isn't it, Mama?" said Ephah.

"There is much evil there," she said. "Babylon is fallen, fallen, that great city. Do you remember the Book of Revelations?"

"Not all of it," I said lamely.

"I taught myself to read the Bible," she said. "The Lord showed me how. No one ever taught me how to read, not a single day of school in my life. But one day, when I was ready to, when the Lord gave me the grace to, I picked up the Bible and I knew what the letters were. There's learnin' in my family—my grandmother was an educated woman. But the only readin' I ever needed was the words as come from the Lord, an' he wanted me to know the letters to read 'em."

Shiphrah slid a Bible in front of her mother—an old family Bible, with an ornate embossed leather binding.

She opened it to the page she wanted, exactly there. She did not have to flip over as much as one page to get to it.

She began to read a very strange passage, the kind of thing I used to hear the preacher read when I was little and still had to go to church, and that I never could believe was really in the Bible. It was all about a beast with seven heads, and horns, and feet like a bear.

She read in a voice that was exactly like her normal conversational voice; in fact, it was as though she had learned how to speak, as well as to read, from reading the Bible.

"'. . . And he doeth great wonders, so that he maketh fire come down from heaven on the earth in the sight of men.'"

She followed every word on the page in front of her, although I was sure that she knew every word by heart and didn't need to. The baby slept on her shoulder, next to her cheek. I had the feeling that the words of the scripture were penetrating straight into its soul.

"'. . . And he causeth all, both small and great, rich and poor, free and bond, to receive a mark in their right hand, or in their foreheads:

"'And that no man might buy or sell, save that he had the mark, or the name of the beast, or the number of his name.'"

She looked up from the book. "The Lord called me up into the mountains to get away from the mark of the beast," she said. "They put it on you down there.

Numbers. Social Security numbers, income tax numbers, telephone numbers."

She took a comb out of her apron and began to run it through her long, fine hair. She worked slowly, starting with the part in the center of the scalp and making short but fluid strokes with the broken-toothed comb, patient and unhurried, rocking and combing until each hair lay flat and straight.

"There's somethin' wrong with Jim Otis Churchwarden, even livin' up here as long as he has. And that's been a long time—but he went away, and when he came back it was a mockery, and it's been a mockery as long's he's been back—'and deceiveth them that dwell on the earth, by means of those miracles which he had the power to do in the sight of the beast.' But he never could deceive me. There's somethin' evil inside him, somethin' that takes pleasure in destruction."

"You've known him a long time, then?"

A faraway look came into her eyes. She seemed to be wrestling with memories or thoughts that she was trying to push away. Un-Biblical thoughts, maybe. I didn't know.

"Jim Otis was sent as a tribulation to me, for my sins, though I say it as shouldn't," she said suddenly.

I didn't understand what she was talking about. I looked at the children, but they averted their eyes. Could this totally devout woman have had an affair with Jim Otis Churchwarden? It was hard to believe— easier to imagine that he'd violated her somehow. But wouldn't her husband have gone after him, then? It must be a secret that she kept locked within herself.

"He's hunting me down now, like an animal," I said. "I have to find a way back to civilization."

"He could do that," she mused. "He has it in him." She paused for a moment, and appeared to be uncertain as to how to go on—the first time I had seen her that way. "There have been those as tried to change him, to teach him, but his heart has always loved mischief and destruction."

"Can you help me get away from him?" I asked. "Can you show me the way back to civilization?"

"Civilization? Yes, I can show you."

"Can you take me?"

"No. I never leave the mountain, not for anything. But I will show you. Now ye'll need rest here tonight, and we can talk more in the morning."

"You didn't finish readin' the lesson, Ma," said Ephah.

"That's enough for tonight," she said.

She gave me a pallet on the floor, and the family prepared for bed, too. We would all sleep in the one room of the cabin. Mrs. Johnson blew out the light and began to get herself ready for bed.

The full moonlight was bright enough so that even in the dark I could see her plainly, in silhouette, taking off her outer garments and putting on her nightdress.

And I realized then, at least in part, why all her Bible-centered, Fundamentalist religious ideas and expressions had not made me feel nervous and uncomfortable. It was because they were natural, as natural as her sensuality. Her physical presence and her spiritual presence were one and the same; she was womanly and graceful, and her breasts swung from side to side like bells in the moonlight.

I looked over at Shiphrah, already lying with her eyes closed on the other bed, which she shared with her eight-year-old brother, after saying her prayers. She had been thirteen or fourteen, and had been lying as she lay now, when just across the room from her, her father and mother had conceived the baby that was Mizraim. I thought about Carolee again, and then I fell asleep.

CHAPTER 14

It was as though I had never met Mrs. Johnson and her children, and as though there were no cabin with a picket fence around it tucked away anywhere in the mountains. Two hundred yards away, and over a ridge, the forest looked the way it had looked for days, before I had seen the cabin or guessed at its existence.

But I was fed now, and rested, and I had Mrs. Johnson's directions on how to get out of the mountains and down into town.

And she had given me a prophecy out of the Bible, opening the book at random and letting her finger fall on the page, then reading me what it said:

" 'The Lord that delivered me out of the paw of the lion, and out of the paw of the bear, He will deliver me out of the hand of this Philistine.' "

"I hope you're right," I said.

"It ain't me, it is the Lord," she said. "And He is always right. Do you know where that passage come from?"

"No, uh . . . not exactly. It's awfully familiar, though."

"It comes from the story of David and Goliath."

"Well, that's encouraging—I guess. But Goliath wasn't stalking David through the woods with a high-powered rifle. At least he had a chance to face him."

"If'n the Lord thought that was tribulation enough for David, I reckon it was. And ye'll get that chance. Jim Otis'll face ye down in the end, after he's tracked ye an' terrorized ye until he gets his fill of it. He'll want that, at the end. And if ye let the fear come over you, like you were doin' last night, ye won't have a chance against him. 'Fear came upon me, and trembling.' And it's that fear as Jim Otis'll be countin' on, he will count on it that your fear will be such that when he shows himself to ye, ye'll think that he is invincible. That is the advantage his kind always take for themselves—'And all the men of Israel, when they saw Goliath, fled from him, and were sore afraid.'"

"I'm afraid he'll be right," I said. "I will be afraid."

"Ye've been afraid of Jim Otis Churchwarden for a long time," she said.

"All my life," I admitted.

"Fear God," she said. "Take the Lord with you. I'll be prayin' for your deliverance and for your soul."

For my soul? I had an uneasy feeling that she might be hedging her bet on her prayers for my deliverance.

I didn't know what difference it would make when I got to the point of looking down Jim Otis' gun barrel, but all things being equal, I supposed I would rather have Mrs. Johnson praying for me than against me.

And I thought she might be right: if Jim Otis had gone on playing this long, he must want a showdown

for the finish of it. That was in keeping with his sense
of the dramatic, his sense of humor, and his sense of
superiority.

If I kept my head, I might have a chance—certainly,
I'd have no chance at all if I didn't.

It wasn't easy. I still felt watched, and of course I
had no guarantee that he wouldn't just knock me off
at any time, when the whim struck him, in spite of
Mrs. Johnson's theories.

The important thing was not to panic. Being rested
helped: every snapping twig no longer sounded like a
gunshot, every tree no longer had the malevolent aura
of a being that existed for the sole purpose of deliberately shielding a killer.

Where would it be, the confrontation? Where would
he show himself? Maybe I should just sit down under
a tree and let him come to me. That would be better
than just letting him have a wide-open choice of his
own time or place.

But my nerves couldn't handle it. He'd hold out
much better than I would, over a long wait. My only
course was to keep going. At least if I kept on the trail
out of the mountains, he'd be forced to show his hand
eventually—either that, or let me excape.

The trail that Mrs. Johnson had mapped out for me
ran about half a mile north of the cabin. I tried not to
think much about that, until the landscape around
me started looking too familiar; and then, try as I
might, I couldn't resist the temptation to make a de-
tour south, close enough to look at it.

I came around on a ridge that gave me a close,

unobstructed, and yet well-hidden view of the cabin. I had a sinking, angry, jealous feeling of anticipation in my stomach, wondering if I would see Jim Otis down there with Carolee.

I suppose I was half disappointed when I didn't.

When I peeped over the ridge, in fact, there was no one in sight at all. That may have been just as well: the cabin all by itself was emotional jolt enough, for a start.

There was a column of smoke coming from the chimney, starting straight up and then being blown in the direction away from me by a gentle but steady breeze. I wondered if there was coffee on the stove, and fresh flowers in the whiskey jug on the table.

I had been watching the house for about twenty minutes, lying stretched out on my stomach, disturbing and elusive thoughts flitting through my head, when Carolee came out. She had laundry with her, and was on her way to hang it up.

She looked different. In spite of the fact that I had been waiting for her, that she was the person I had been expecting to see, it was almost as if I didn't recognize her at first. It was as though she were someone I remembered rather than knew.

The laundry was all her own. Underwear, sweatshirt, pair of jeans. Not very much. A vagrant thought popped into my head: I wondered if she was pregnant.

I thought about Mrs. Johnson's Mark of the Beast. Numbers. Social Security numbers, telephone numbers. Everyone down in the cities was corrupted by them, numbers that were assigned to them, emblazoned on their foreheads. "And no man might buy or sell, save that he had the mark, or the name of the beast, or the number of his name." I wondered if ages were another part of the Mark of the Beast that got emblazoned on people.

Mrs. Johnson had given food and shelter to Jim Otis, too. Right after the building had fallen down, he had shown up there. And she had invited him in, too, even knowing what happened, knowing that he had been shooting at another human being out in the woods, even knowing how evil he was.

" 'I was naked, and ye clothed me,' " she said. "Of course, I took him in. 'The heart is deceitful above all things, and desperately wicked: who can know it?' "

I wondered how old Mrs. Johnson had been when she got married. I couldn't even begin to guess, any more than I could begin to guess how old she was now. I thought about her daughter, Shiphrah, growing up in her own body, lying in her bed at night next to her brother and listening to her parents across the room, making a baby. And Ephah, the little boy, eight years old, lying next to his teenage sister, listening.

I had never conceived of my parents making love, when I was eight years old. I still couldn't imagine it, in fact. I had shared a room with my brothers, my sisters had shared their own room, and my parents' door was always closed. Maybe that was what had stopped me from being of the real mountain folk.

I wondered, if he had been there, if Mr. and Mrs. Johnson would have made love in front of me. No, it was too late. Nobody would ever make love in front of me. Not unless you counted some horny exhibitionist at a party in Washington, sometime, if I ever got back.

I tried to imagine myself living in a one-room shack, making love to Carolee while the children slept on the other side of the room.

No. Nothing was natural to me.

Carolee had seen horses and pigs mount each other; had seen calves being born, goats castrated. (They say the best way is to bite the goat's balls off.) Her family was as poor and as large as any in the county; they couldn't have lived in much more than one room, either. She had to have listened to her parents making love. Her sister Leona must have, too. I wondered if Carolee had ever seen anyone being killed; had ever seen anyone die.

I never had. I realized it with a start. I had no experience there, either.

I had never seen anyone being born; had never seen anyone make love; had never seen anyone die.

I had seen the pictures. I had seen the pictures of Leona and her boyfriend with their lower halves coupled and their upper halves blown away. I had talked knowledgeably about it with the state troopers, and I had somehow assumed that all of that made me an authority, and that it somehow gave me license to dictate how people ought to respond to one another.

Carolee looked up at the sky, one hand on her hip, the other shading her eyes. It was gray. It could rain— maybe even snow a little if it got cold enough by nightfall. Then she picked up her empty laundry basket and went back inside, and I cursed not seeing her anymore.

I stood up. I had gotten a little stiff, lying in one

position for so long. I walked back to the trail Mrs. Johnson had directed me to.

I wasn't sure how much further I had to go—a full day's walk to the nearest house, Mrs. Johnson had said, dawn to dark. And of course I wasn't sure how much of that distance I'd be permitted to travel.

Today was the first time since I'd been out in the woods that I'd thought of anything more than my immediate peril. It was a good thing to do. I was less anxious, less tense, less panic-driven. More alert, too, as long as I didn't permit my mind to wander too far into other thoughts. I was in just the frame of mind that Mrs. Johnson had advised me to cultivate, and I felt ready for anything.

But the farther I walked away from Carolee's cabin, the more insecure I began to feel. I knew that if I were just to keep walking, waiting for Jim Otis to make his move, it would get worse and worse.

I had to bring him to me, somehow—I had to choose a spot to make my stand and then find a way to provoke him to come to me.

I hit upon a plan.

I turned and went northward through the woods. I started walking briskly, but before long I broke into a run.

The excitement was building up in me: excitement and hatred. I hated Jim Otis so much! I hated him more than I had ever felt any emotion before—I wanted to kill him, to crush, to destroy, to inflict pain and suffering on him; I wanted to strike him and hurt him in any way I could.

I didn't know where Jim Otis was now. I knew he

must be close at hand, but I ran faster and faster, staggering and stumbling at times, but going as fast as I could, extending my body beyond its limits. I was panting and gasping for breath when I crashed into the clearing where Jim Otis' still was located, but my anger kept me going.

I wished I had an axe or a sledgehammer, but my rage was enough of an implement of destruction. I kicked and shook the scaffolding that held the second still, until it collapsed and the tank crashed to the ground, breaking one of the copper tubes that connected to it and bending the other one out of shape. I kicked it again and again on the ground, until finally the other piece of tubing snapped and rolled down into the stream.

I took out my Bowie knife and stabbed at the copper box repeatedly, turning it into a sieve; then I pushed it off its platform and stabbed it some more. I kicked over the copper condenser and stomped on it repeatedly, crushing the soft metal.

I wanted nothing left standing, nothing left reparable. I knocked over the hot-water heater that served as the second condenser, pried the top off with my knife, and pulled out the copper coil. Then, swinging that by one end, I pounded it against the rocks until it was flattened and useless.

Standing back about ten paces, I shot the pressure gauge off the top of the boiler. Then I picked up the heaviest boulder I could lift above my head, and smashed it down at the base of the boiler where it was embedded in the firebox. About four blows of the boulder was all it took to crack the bricks and begin to dislodge the tank; three more blows, and it was ripped loose completely.

Excitement was still bubbling up in me when I had finished, but I felt cool and composed. I sat down on a rock, wiped my forehead with my sleeve, and waited for Jim Otis.

I knew I wouldn't hear him as he came up. And I knew that he wouldn't shoot at me from ambush, not now—he'd have to face me, first. So I wasn't tense or fearful as I waited, and I wasn't straining my eyes and ears for signs of his approach.

Instead, I became aware, as if for the first time, of the woods, cool and blue-green in the shade, bright and glinting in the sunlight. The rocks had green and gray lichen patterns on them, and the fallen trees had a darker green moss. The dead trunks of fallen pine had rings of knots where branches had once grown symmetrically; hardwood trunks lying near them had the remnants of haphazardly sprouted branches. The sky was blue and bleached by the sun, almost white. I could hear the harsh but suddenly beautiful cry of a crow from high in the trees. And then Jim Otis stepped out into the clearing.

It was a shock to see him. He had been an unseen presence for such a long time, it was as though I had never been face to face with him before. I had to absorb each detail of his features, as if for the first time.

He didn't look as crazy as I'd expected him to— maybe not as crazy as I looked, at that moment. He didn't even look savage.

Jim Otis Churchwarden. Height: five feet, eleven inches. Dark hair thinning just a little in front, hairline just starting to recede, but sideburns as full and black as ever. Little brush mustache, dark straight eyebrows with twinkling dark eyes under them. Full lips, for a narrow face, and they curled back over almost even teeth (one gold one) in an easygoing grin.

It was like a face I'd seen in a magazine, or on a reward poster, or in a dream, or on someone else. But gradually it began to look familiar again. Just old Cousin Jim Otis Churchwarden, with the easy smile and the always-engaging manner.

"Hey, there, Cousin Ry," he drawled. "What kinda hodge-menage we got ourselves here, hey?"

As I got used to looking at him again, I found I was seeing him for the first time. I was looking beyond that twinkle in his eyes, to a fixed stare that never left them. Yes, and the twinkle was just a reflection of that dead stare. It would always glimmer there, whether there was any reason for its being there or not. That ingratiating grin, that fun-loving, friendly twinkle must have been on his lips and in his eyes when he leaped up on the hood of that Mercury, and shot Leona Blye Churchwarden and her boyfriend. It must have been the last thing that she saw.

And it might be the last thing that I saw.

The lilt in his voice was, as always, an invitation to join him in his mood: *'Tain't serious, Cousin, it's just us good ol' boys together, let's unbutton our vests, have a shot o' white lightnin', an' laugh about it all.* I kept my voice level, and dead serious.

"I broke up your still, Jim Otis," I said.

"Well, you know, you hadn't ought to of done that, Cousin," he said, still grinning. "That was a mighty nice still, now. Took me a long time to put it together. Finest still I ever owned."

"I did, though. I broke your fucking still. I broke it all to hell, you bastard."

"Well, now, if that don't beat all. An' here I take you out in the woods, an' teach you all about huntin' . . . an' trackin' . . ."

I stared at him through eyes steady and narrow with hatred, coldly refusing his bantering. I wanted to cut through that facade and expose the viciousness of his real nature. Even if no one ever saw it but me, I wanted it to happen.

But I knew that was impossible. It would never happen. There was just nothing else there, nothing under the smile. To himself, Jim Otis was his mask—he was always, would always be, the big kid impressing the little kids, the scapegrace, the show-off. Whatever he did, however far he went, whatever atrocities he committed, it was all just part of being the lovable rogue and nothing could make him other than that in his own mind.

"I surely did," he said. "I took you out in the woods and showed you purty damn near everything I know, Cousin. Now I don't just do that for everyone, hey? Hell, no. Just my favorite people, kinfolk an' suchlike."

"Was Leona one of your favorite people?" I asked.

There was venom in my voice, but he rode right over it. Not even a flicker of defensiveness clouded his eyes.

"Leona? Hell, now, Cousin, I sure did love that li'l ol' gal. Cute li'l ol' thing, she was, an' she knew what was to happen did she go foolin' around on ol' Jim

Otis. Wham, bam, up on the hood, you ought to a' seen the look in their faces!"

He cackled delightedly at the memory.

"Why did she leave you?"

"Well, Cousin, you know how women are. She didn't have no reason; she just up an' took off one day."

I knew how Carolee was. I hadn't known Leona, and maybe there was no similarity at all between them; but I still wondered what it was that Leona had found too much to handle. I asked the question again, biting the words off more viciously this time.

"Why did she leave you?"

"Aw, shit, Cousin, you know." He still was not at all perturbed; he just seemed good-humoredly embarrassed at admitting a few peccadilloes he was secretly proud of—*Come on, Jim Otis, tell us about the time you put the tack on the teacher's chair.*

"She just said she figgered I was too crazy for her an' all. Couldn't get used to a little teasin' an' funnin' an' suchlike. Guess she wanted to change me, you know."

Something didn't ring true, but I didn't know quite what or why. " 'Teasin' and funnin' '?" I asked. "Like what you've been doing with me?"

"Well, shucks, Cousin, you been a purty good sport up to now. We had a pretty good time for ourselves out there, hey?"

It was awfully convincing. Even now, he almost was able to get me believing that he hadn't really been trying to kill me, and that he wasn't planning to kill me now. He almost had me believing that the whole thing had been a good-natured romp. Even worse, he almost had me believing that if he did kill me, it would still just be part of a good-natured romp.

There was no way that anyone could talk themselves out of the fact that Jim Otis had killed Leona. My mother couldn't, Carolee couldn't, nobody. But they all could, easily enough, talk themselves into believing that the killing wasn't the main point—that things between Jim Otis and Leona had just gotten out of hand a little bit, but that he hadn't really meant to do it, that he wouldn't deliberately do anything bad.

But I knew it was just the other way around. The killing *was* the main point; the fact that Jim Otis had no limits and no sense that there was anything he couldn't get away with was the main point. He could never feel that he had gone too far, and he had the con man's charm to convince other people of it, so that they always were willing to make up mitigating circumstances for him.

It was different when you were on the other end of his gun. It was hard to make up mitigating circumstances for your own murder.

Mrs. Johnson hadn't been taken in by him, not for a second. I was sure of that. But she had taken him in, taken him into her home, given him food and shelter. Was it just Christian charity? "The heart is deceitful above all things, and desperately wicked; who can know it?" she had said, and I had not understood what she was talking about, except that it was a quotation from the Bible. She couldn't have been using it as an excuse for giving her hospitality to Jim Otis, because she did know it.

"It wasn't a good time, Jim Otis. You know what you were trying to do."

"What *I* was trying to do? Hey, *you're* the one broke *my* still, right? I oughta be mad at you. I just didn't think that was nice at all. No kind o' way to ree-pay my good friendship an' openin' up my cabin to you, findin' you a nice li'l ol' girl friend an' all. An' then you go an' knock down my big ol' house, too, slippin' an' slidin' all over it."

"God damn it, you lying bastard! You *are* totally evil."

For a second, a different look—a strange one—flickered over his face, only to be superseded again by the familiar grin. But not completely, this time.

"Evil, is it, now? Oh, yeah, that's right—you been talkin' to Mrs. Johnson, ain't you?"

I only glared at him.

"Fine woman, Mrs. Johnson. Real good woman, you'd have to say. Wouldn't you have to say that, now, Cousin?"

I said nothing.

"Sure you would. A good woman. Knows all about the Lord, knows how to get saved, knows how to pray for folks. She tell you 'bout prayin' that li'l boy's scars away?"

"Yes."

"That's true, you know. Saw 'em myself, with my own two eyes, all them nasty big ol' red scars. Guess the Lord must 'a been somewhere watchin' a sparrow when he got burnt, but Mrs. Johnson sure took care o' prayin' him up after it happened."

There was something funny, an especially mocking

twist to the way Jim Otis pronounced Mrs. Johnson's name. He paused now, and seemed to be studying my face, to see if I was suitably impressed.

"That's PRETTY GOOD, AIN'T IT?" he bellowed suddenly.

"Yeah. Sure," I said, startled.

"Yessir, she is good, all right. But she warn't always good, did you know that, Cousin?"

"No," I said. "I didn't know it."

"Nope. She turned good. Lord come an' talked to her, guv her all them gifts, brung her up on the mountaintop. But she had desires, too, when she's a young 'un. Desires o' the flesh. Oh, an' she submitted to 'em. Real young, too, and ol' Lord caught her up on it. Baby out o' wedlock. Oh, the disgrace of it all. Family never did live it down. Forever an' ever after, a blot on the good name o' Churchwarden."

"Churchwarden!" The name hit me, and bounced back out of my mouth like an echo. I knew Jim Otis had been raised by his grandparents—lots of people said that was why he turned out so wild.

"Yep," said Jim Otis. "It was . . ."

There was a different look on Jim Otis' face now—what, for him, almost passed for introspection. That strange look had come back.

". . . It was Churchwarden Manor, the big ol' house you knocked down. When me an' Ma lived up in the mountains together, when we lived in the moonshinin' cabin back when I was just a tad, I used to run away all the time; go an' hide in that big ol' house. Ma finally had to come down out o' the mountains, send me to live with my granddaddy. Then she—"

I was fascinated, almost hypnotized, by his story. I wanted it to go on. But a reflex in me shouted *Now!* And I knew that his moment of distraction would not last long. I brought up my gun and fired.

I had no time to brace myself, and the recoil knocked me backward. I struck my shoulder and the side of my head against the ground.

I scrambled back up, half dazed, not knowing whether or not I would be taking my last look down the barrel of Jim Otis' rifle. But the weapon lay harmless, three feet away from him on the ground. His right arm was dangling at an awkward, useless angle, and blood was spurting from a severed artery in it.

And his face had lost its grin at last, and for good. The twinkle had faded from his eyes, replaced by bewilderment, then disbelief, then gradually expanding horror that this could have happened to him— that he was not invulnerable.

He howled with pain and rage. Then he turned and ran into the woods.

It took a couple of minutes for my head to clear. I had landed hard on the ground, and my shoulder was still throbbing. By the time I was able to get up and chase him, he was gone. He had picked up his gun and taken it with him, so I didn't want to follow too recklessly.

But he was badly wounded, and he wouldn't get far. And I was suddenly tired, sick and tired. And I wanted to see Carolee.

CHAPTER 15

She sank the axe into a stump and turned around as she heard me approach. We stood about ten feet apart, looking at each other.

"I hoped you'd come back," she said at last.

"But you knew one of us would," I said, without bitterness.

"I heard a shot nearby," she said. "Couple—three days ago, there was a lot of shots, but they was farther away. Didn't hear nothin' after that. That was scary. So much shootin', I figured something must of happened. Last couple o' days I been real worried."

"That no one would come and get you, and you'd be stuck up here?"

"I was worried about you."

"Well . . . I'm all right."

She gave me a wide, sunny smile to show how pleased she was. Then at last, I started toward her and she toward me. We hugged each other, and she put her face up to be kissed.

I took her hand and started for the house.

"Ry! It's the middle of the day!" she protested, but she came with me.

I fell asleep right after we made love, and slept the rest of the day. Carolee got up, but in periods of semi-wakefulness I was aware that she came and looked in on me every so often during the course of the afternoon.

It was nearly dark when I finally woke up. I lay in bed with my eyes open, and waited for Carolee. I could hear her moving around out in the other room, and I thought of calling out to her, but it was nicer to wait. It was nicer to just lie quietly in the dark, in the blissful, imcomparable comfort of that lumpy mattress, and listen to the sounds of life going on in the room on the other side of the door. And she would be coming in again, I could be sure of that. There was no hurry anymore—no urgency, no fear hanging over me. I could just lie back, and listen, and wait.

She came in soon enough. I hadn't even begun to grow impatient yet. She looked twice, and when she was sure that I was really awake, she came over and sat down on the bed, next to me.

"Feelin' better?"

"Yeah."

"Get a good rest?"

"Sure did."

She bent over and kissed me lightly. I took her hand, and held it. I began to think consciously, for the first time, about being in love with her, wondering if I was or not. I guessed that I was. I didn't let myself carry on that line of speculation much futher. I didn't want to know what it meant, what I was going to do about it.

"I'm . . . I'm glad you're all right," she said.

"Me, too," I said.

"And . . . Jim Otis?"

"He's wounded." I told her about the final gun duel. "He ran off into the woods, and I couldn't find him. But he's pretty badly hurt, I'd guess. He won't be able to go too far, or do too much."

"What are you going to do about him?"

"Nothing, now. He'll keep. In the morning I'm going back into town for help. There's no point following after him, because he's probably holed up someplace—and even wounded, with a gun he's still dangerous."

"Suppose he's hurt . . . real bad? Suppose he needs help?"

"There's nothing I can do about that. I'll have the troopers bring a doctor with them when they come back. I'm not risking my life out there again just to see if he needs first aid."

"You're right," she said. I looked at her face for any signs of disapproval, but there were none. She did think I was right. I appreciated that, although at the same time it made me wonder if perhaps I was wrong.

"I should be able to make it down into town safely," I said. "I don't think he can use his right arm at all. He won't be able to set up much of an ambush."

"When will you be leavin'?"

"In the morning. I can take you down with me, since there won't be any danger."

"No!"

The word broke out of her involuntarily. She

stopped, and tried to steady herself, but her head hung, and she was not far from tears.

"I don't wanta."

"But you have to. If it weren't tomorrow it would just be the next day, when I get back, or the day after."

"I don't wanta ever go back down there. I got nothing down there to go to."

She was glaring at me now, as if I were an enemy.

"I know, Carolee. But it wouldn't have been any better if Jim Otis had made it and I hadn't. You still couldn't have stayed."

The glare faded from her eyes, and she looked miserable again. "I know, I know," she said. "I know it wouldn't of. I didn't want that to happen, nohow. I never did! Well, maybe for a second just now, when you said what you said, but not really. I'm glad you're all right—I'm awful glad." She ended in a burst of sobs.

I reached out and gathered her close to me. She sobbed some more, pressing her clenched fists against my chest. I felt all-powerful and helpless at the same time. She sobbed for a while in my arms, then pulled away and finished sobbing while she sat on the edge of the bed, her head in her hands.

"What . . . what'll happen then?" she asked.

"We'll worry about that when the time comes," I said. "Come to bed now."

"Yes," she said. "It's still our house tonight, anyhow." She snuggled up to me under the covers.

"While you were gone I sewed up some real curtains for the kitchen windows," she said. "You prob'ly didn't

even notice 'em when you come in, you were so tired.
Anyway, you'll see 'em in the mornin'. I found a old
. . . I dunno, bedspread, I guess it was, or some
kinda light blanket. Dunno where it come from, but it
was kinda pretty, pretty enough, an' I just whupped
'em up outa that. An' I changed the whole kitchen
around, you can really work in it now. I tell you, it
was just plain ridiculous the way Jim Otis had it fixed
up, couldn't find nothin', nothin' next to what it
should be next to—"

"Carolee, there can't be more than about two pots
and a couple of spoons in that whole kitchen," I said.

"Well, that's true enough, there ain't too much.
That's why it's so important to have it all set up right.
It's hard enough, workin' in a kitchen as don't have
hardly nothin' to work with, 'thout havin' it all confused, too."

"What else did you do?" I asked.

"Well, I sure split a bunch o' logs," she said. "Bet
we got enough wood split now to make it through
pretty near the whole winter, cookin' an' heatin' both."

"That's good," I said.

"It ain't hard to find enough to do when you ain't
got a man around," she said. "Even up here, where I
didn't bring much stuff with me. I like to do things. I
like to keep busy."

"What sort of things do you like to do?"

"Oh, things. Sewin', an' quiltin', that sort o' stuff.
Just to keep my hands busy. I like to take long walks
in the woods, too, an' think. 'Course I didn't do much
o' that these last days. Truth to tell, I was pretty

scared o' walkin' around in these woods, with all that crazy shootin' goin' on."

"What do you think about, when you take your long walks?"

"Oh, things. People. What I'd like to do, places I'd like to go."

"What sort of places? Where would you like to go?"

"Oh, wow, I dunno. Places like . . . you know, far-away places. Paris, France. Places they told us about in school, that I read about in school."

"Do you read much?" I asked.

"Not much."

"It's a good way to learn about faraway places."

"Oh, I guess I don't care about faraway places all that much. I . . . oh, Ry!"

She broke off in a sob, and hugged me tightly, covering my chest, shoulders, and face with kisses.

I wanted to make love to Carolee forever. I wanted to make love to her all night long, just never stop until I had to—until morning came and it was time to go, time to go into town and get the troopers.

That was when we heard the crash of the outer door opening.

I only had a few seconds to react, just the time it took for about five stumbling steps in the outer room; and then the bedroom door burst open with a crash.

Pain and shock had driven all the laughter far out of Jim Otis' eyes. They were hollow now, and feverish, and his face was contorted with tension. His right arm, wrapped in a blood-soaked piece of cloth, hung limply by his side, but he held his gun steady by pressing it against his body with his left elbow. His left index finger was on the trigger. He leaned heavily against the doorway.

Carolee sat bolt upright in bed, clutching the blanket in front of her. I sat up also, but that put me directly behind her.

"Don't point that gun at me, you crazy man!" she hissed. "Don't you come around me with no guns."

Jim Otis gestured at her with the gun barrel. The movement was more wobbly than he meant it to be. When he spoke, his voice was slurred and thick.

"Better . . . ge' outa there, you fuckin' bitch. Jes' as soon kill you, too, like your sister. Cheap whore, jes' like . . . Leona. I know you."

"Yah, Leona told me about you, Jim Otis Churchwarden. She told me you wasn't no man. That's why she left you."

Jim Otis gave a roar of pain and anger, that ended in a sob. "What did she know . . . dumb little kid . . . what call did she have to want no . . ."

"Yeah, that's why you married her, ain't it? Little girl, hey? She come into your house, into your bed; that made her a woman in her eyes. And in the world's eyes, too, and you wasn't no man! Wha'd you expect her to do but leave you? An' wha'd you expect when she left you, everyone lookin' at her like a woman then? Yeah, maybe she even still loved you, but wha'd you expect?"

Jim Otis' eyes were leaden. I was afraid for a moment that he was going to shoot Carolee, but he only had one shot left in him. He was too weak to stand up to the recoil. And he wanted that shot for me.

"Get outa there an' put your clothes on . . . whore!" he roared.

She stared at him without saying a word; then, after a moment, she got slowly out of bed, covering herself as best she could with her hands. She walked sideways over to the corner of the room where she had left her clothes.

Jim Otis leaned forward, the gun now trained directly on me.

"Thought . . . you'd seen the last of ol' Jim Otis, hey? Thought you'd kilt me, run off an' left me for dead? *Run off an' left ol' Jim Otis for dead?*"

"I didn't—I would have tried to follow you . . ." I began.

"Yeh, an' I know . . . I know wha' that's all about, too. Ol' Jim Otis ain't gonna let . . . ain't gonna . . ."

His eyes glazed over, and his head bowed, but he recovered himself. He couldn't hold on much longer, but he could hold on long enough to finish me off.

I didn't see that there was anything I could do to stop him. His reflexes couldn't be very fast anymore; but even so, there was no possible way that I could make a lunge for him. My feet were tangled in the blanket, and it would trip me up if I tried to leap out of bed.

"You can't . . . do nothin' like that to ol' Jim Otis . . ." he croaked. I didn't know what he meant; he was rambling. "Nobody can . . . you are gonna die now for sure, Cousin Ry, die for sure—no playin' no games now, no havin' no more fun . . . die for sure . . ."

"Look, Jim Otis," I said. "You're hurt bad—you need

help. Let me take care of you, get you medical attention—"

He let out an unearthly sound. I don't know if it was meant to be a laugh—I think so. There was more pain in it than anything else.

"You!" he shrieked, his voice cracking. "You? Fuckin' snot-nosed kid . . . nobody takes care o' Jim Otis . . . you gonna . . . die for . . . sure. . . ."

He leaned further forward, dangerously close to falling. But the gun was still steady in his hand. His eyes were glazed, but I could read the look in them— the unmistakable look that told me this was it: he was about to pull the trigger.

I was beyond terror. I felt nothing. Nothing, except that everything was happening very slowly.

But when the explosion came, it came from somewhere else. And Jim Otis' body suddenly went erect, his arms were flung out from his sides, he spun around hard and smashed into the wall.

Then he slid down it.

Carolee stood against the wall that the rifle's kick had thrown her into, the gun in her hand, and an intense expression still knotting her face.

"You come into my house . . ." she hissed at the corpse. "Come into my house with a gun . . ."

She stood rigid, and her eyes still blazed with indignation. She held the gun pointed at Jim Otis' corpse as though she expected it to leap back to life and threaten her home again. She held it steady, and her whole being stayed charged with passion for so long that I thought she was going to start pumping more bullets into him.

I made a move toward her, and she dropped the gun as though she had just discovered she was holding it, and ran toward me. I stood up to meet her, and took her in my arms.

She sobbed uncontrollably, burying her head on my chest.

"Jim Otis is dead," she said.

"Yes, he's dead."

"We'll be . . . goin' back down in the morning."

I nodded, though she was not looking up at me.

"An' you . . ."

I stood dumbly, not even nodding.

"Can you . . . take him away? Out of . . . the house?"

"Yeah," I said, forcing the words out as though I had not spoken in a long time, and had lost the habit.

"An' then . . . come back an' stay with me?"

"Yeah."

I put on my pants, picked up the body under the armpits, and began dragging it slowly toward the door.

MORE SAVAGE — MORE SHOCKING than Helter Skelter!

THE GANG

by Herbert Kastle
author of <u>Cross-Country</u> and <u>Ellie</u>

THEY WERE HER MEN:

• Bert, a writer who was determined to turn his fictional fantasies into hard action for the first time in his life.

• Manny, a big, handsome stud going downhill, desperate to prove his manhood again.

• Mark, Manny's teen-age son, who crossed over the generation gap to join his elders in a world of x-rated kicks and kills.

SHE WAS THEIR WOMAN:

• Celia, six feet of breath-taking female, dedicated to satisfying every passion of these three men, so long as she could hold them together.

THEY WERE THE GANG
Bound together by violent lust and hate, no law of God or man could stop them!

A DELL BOOK $1.95   (2786-06)

At your local bookstore or use this handy coupon for ordering:

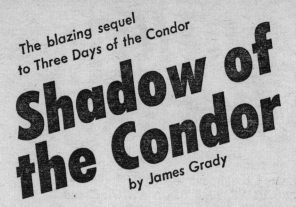

BESTSELLERS
FROM DELL

fiction

- [ ] THE CHOIRBOYS by Joseph Wambaugh $2.25 (1188-10)
- [ ] NIGHTWORK by Irwin Shaw $1.95 (6460-00)
- [ ] SHOGUN by James Clavell $2.75 (7800-15)
- [ ] MARATHON MAN by William Goldman..... $1.95 (5502-02)
- [ ] WHERE ARE THE CHILDREN? by Mary H. Clark $1.95 (9593-04)
- [ ] RICH MAN, POOR MAN by Irwin Shaw $1.95 (7424-29)
- [ ] THE GARGOYLE CONSPIRACY
      by Marvin H. Alpert $1.95 (5239-02)
- [ ] GHOSTBOAT
      by George Simpson and Neal Burger $1.95 (5421-00)
- [ ] DISTURBING THE PEACE by Richard Yates ... $1.95 (1797-13)

non-fiction

- [ ] BRING ON THE EMPTY HORSES
      by David Niven $1.95 (0824-04)
- [ ] MIRACLES OF THE GODS
      by Erich von Däniken $1.95 (5594-19)
- [ ] BREACH OF FAITH by Theodore H. White .. $1.95 (0780-14)
- [ ] JUDY by Gerold Frank $2.50 (5107-01)
- [ ] DR. SIEGAL'S NATURAL FIBER PERMANENT
      WEIGHT-LOSS DIET
      by Sanford Siegal, D.O., M.D. $1.75 (7790-25)
- [ ] EST: Playing the Game the New Way
      by Carl Frederick $3.95 (2365-13)
- [ ] THREE ON A DATE by Stephanie Buffington .. $1.50 (5078-06)
- [ ] BELLEVUE by Don Gold $1.95 (0473-16)

Buy them at your local bookstore or use this handy coupon for ordering:

Dell **DELL BOOKS**
P.O. BOX 1000, PINEBROOK, N.J. 07058

Please send me the books I have checked above. I am enclosing $_____
(please add 35¢ per copy to cover postage and handling). Send check or money
order—no cash or C.O.D.'s. Please allow up to 8 weeks for shipment.

Mr/Mrs/Miss_____

Address_____

City_____State/Zip_____